The
Babysitting
Wars

candy apple books...
just for you.
sweet. fresh. fun.
take a bite!

The Accidental Cheerleader
by Mimi McCoy

The Boy Next Door
by Laura Dower

Miss Popularity
by Francesco Sedita

How to Be a Girly Girl in Just Ten Days
by Lisa Papademetriou

Drama Queen
by Lara Bergen

The Babysitting Wars

by MIMI McCOY

candy
apple

SCHOLASTIC INC.

New York Toronto London Auckland Sydney
Mexico City New Delhi Hong Kong Buenos Aires

ISBN-13: 978-0-439-92954-7
ISBN-10: 0-439-92954-7

Book design by Tim Hall

12 11 10 9 8 7 6 5 4 3 2 1   7 8 9 10 11 12/0
Printed in the U.S.A.   40
First printing, November 2007

For Elyse, with thanks

Chapter One

"Victory!" Kaitlyn Sweeney declared. She strode up to the table in the Marshfield Lake Middle School cafeteria, the fingers of her left hand raised over her head in a *V*.

Her best friends, Liesel and Maggie, looked up from their lunches. Liesel flipped her shaggy blond bangs out of her eyes. "What victory?" she asked.

"I got the last brownie." Kaitlyn held up a walnut-studded square wrapped in plastic.

"Ew, nuts," Liesel said, wrinkling her nose.

Kaitlyn dropped her lunch tray on the table and slid into the seat across from Liesel. "I saw this guy looking at it, so I pretended I was just reaching for a milk. Then, at the last second, I snagged it from right under his nose."

Maggie rolled her eyes. "Kaitlyn, only you could turn buying a brownie into a competitive sport."

"Hey, you snooze, you lose." Kaitlyn unwrapped the brownie. "Anybody want a bite?"

Liesel shook her head. "Walnuts are vile." She'd always been a picky eater. For as long as Kaitlyn had known her — which was pretty much their whole lives — she'd lived mainly on grilled cheese sandwiches and root beer.

"Your loss," Kaitlyn said with a shrug.

"I'll take some," said Maggie, reaching for the brownie.

"Hey, I said a *bite*!"

"Vat wuff a bide," Maggie mumbled through a mouthful.

Maggie was the opposite of Liesel — she ate anything. While Liesel was small, Maggie was tall. She had long black hair that she wore in a braid down her back. Maggie played volleyball and ran on the track and cross-country teams. She had practice every day, and as a result she was *always* hungry.

Kaitlyn was right in between her friends: medium size, medium height, medium-length medium-brown hair. She sometimes joked that the three of them were the perfect set — they came with one in every size.

Kaitlyn polished off the rest of her brownie, then started on a turkey sandwich. Liesel was halfheartedly nibbling at a plate of french fries, and Maggie was working on her second slice of pizza. As she chewed, Kaitlyn glanced around the cafeteria. The sounds of kids' voices bounced off the walls, and the room seemed charged with energy. *Maybe because it's Friday,* Kaitlyn thought. Everyone was excited about the coming weekend.

"Do you guys want to sleep over tomorrow night?" Liesel asked her friends. "My mom has a faculty party at the college, so she won't be home until late. She said we can order pizza."

"I'm in," said Maggie.

"I can't," said Kaitlyn. "I'm babysitting."

"Again?" Liesel heaved an exaggerated sigh.

Kaitlyn looked at her. "What?"

"It's just, you're *always* babysitting lately," Liesel said. "You babysat last Friday *and* last Saturday and the Saturday before that and the Saturday before *that.*"

Kaitlyn couldn't deny it. Just six months before, at the beginning of seventh grade, she'd started babysitting for a few of her mom's friends. Word got out, and suddenly Kaitlyn had more babysitting jobs than she could keep up with.

3

"Well, I can't cancel now," Kaitlyn replied. "I already told them I'd do it."

"I just don't understand why you want to do it in the first place," Liesel said. "Who wants to sit around wiping little kids' noses? Yech!"

"I do it for the stimulating intellectual conversation," Kaitlyn told her. "And the snacks." Her friends laughed.

"Well, are we all still hanging out at my house tonight?" Maggie asked.

"I'm sitting for the Knopfskys right after school," Kaitlyn said, "but I'll be done pretty early. I can be over by seven." She took another bite of her sandwich.

"Good," said Maggie. "You guys have to see this new video game my brother sent me from college. You build a *mall*. Isn't that cool? You get to pick all the stores but you can't make them all clothes stores, even if you want to, because it turns out a mall won't work with just clothes stores and . . ."

Maggie went on talking. But Kaitlyn no longer heard what she was saying, because at that moment she saw Topher Walker get up from the table where he was sitting with the other basketball players.

Topher Walker, star of the eighth-grade basketball team and owner of the dreamiest set of blue-green eyes Kaitlyn had ever seen, was walking toward their table. And he was looking right at her!

Topher approached, his lips curled in a half smile. Kaitlyn had stopped chewing. In fact, she had pretty much stopped breathing.

"Hey," said Topher.

"Hey," Kaitlyn tried to say. But her mouth was still full of turkey sandwich. It came out "haw."

She felt her face go hot with embarrassment. But Topher didn't seem to notice. He continued past her to the vending machines. Over the noise of the cafeteria, Kaitlyn could hear his coins clatter into the slot of a machine.

Kaitlyn began to breathe again. The bite of sandwich had turned into a gluelike paste in her mouth. She swallowed with difficulty.

"Hello!" Liesel snapped her fingers in front of Kaitlyn's face. "Earth to Kaitlyn."

"Huh?" said Kaitlyn.

Maggie glanced past Kaitlyn at Topher. "Give her a chance to recover," she advised Liesel. "She just had another close encounter of the Topher kind."

"He's like Kaitlyn kryptonite," Liesel noted.

"He is not. Don't look! He'll think we're talking about him," Kaitlyn hissed.

"So? We *are* talking about him," said Liesel. But to Kaitlyn's relief, her friends stopped looking.

5

Kaitlyn made a face. "Did I really just show him a whole mouthful of chewed turkey?"

"It was only half chewed," Liesel said, as if that somehow made it better.

"Whatever. Not like I really care," Kaitlyn said.

Liesel and Maggie rolled their eyes.

"I don't know why you don't just admit it," Liesel said. "You've got it bad for Topher."

"I do not," said Kaitlyn. "Just because I think he's cute and smart and great at basketball doesn't mean I *like* him. I mean, it's not like I want to go out with him."

"Ri-i-ight," Liesel said.

"He's always trying to be the best," Kaitlyn went on. "Like in Spanish class, whenever Señora Ramos puts challenge words up on the board, he always tries to beat everyone else to answer them."

Maggie and Liesel started laughing.

"What?" said Kaitlyn.

"That sounds just like you," Liesel told her.

"You're perfect for each other," Maggie teased, her eyes twinkling.

Kaitlyn frowned and folded her arms across her chest. Maybe she did like Topher. But she wasn't going to admit it now. She hated to lose a debate.

Before she could say anything else, Maggie

started to wave to someone across the room. "Hey, Nola!" she shouted.

"Who's Nola?" asked Kaitlyn. She turned to follow Maggie's gaze. A girl with long brown hair was standing at the edge of the cafeteria, holding a lunch tray and looking around uncertainly. She seemed relieved to see Maggie.

"Hi, Maggie," she said as she approached their table.

Maggie invited her to sit down. "These are my friends Kaitlyn and Liesel," she said.

Kaitlyn and Liesel both said hello.

"Nola's in my English class. She just moved here," Maggie added, unnecessarily. Kaitlyn could tell just by looking at her that Nola wasn't from Marshfield Lake. She was wearing a sweater vest over a crisp white shirt and pants with a crease that could have cut through butter. Her hair looked like she had spent a long time blow-drying it. Most kids at Marshfield Lake just wore jeans and T-shirts, and even the kids who spent a lot of time on their hair looked like they didn't.

"She's from California," Maggie added.

"Los Angeles," Nola said quickly, as if she didn't want to be mistaken for someone from some *other* part of California.

"Really?" Liesel perked up. "I've always wanted to go to L.A. I think it would be totally inspiring."

"Liesel's an artist," Maggie explained to Nola. "She's the best in the school."

Liesel shrugged. "I paint. It's no big deal."

"She's just being modest," Maggie told Nola. "Liesel's, like, a genius. She's going to be in this youth art show at the city museum next month. Only three middle schoolers in the whole district were invited. Everyone else is in high school."

"I went to that museum when we moved here," Nola said. "It's nothing like what we have in L.A. I think MOCA is really the best."

"I love mocha, too!" Maggie enthused. "Though my mom says I shouldn't drink coffee because it stunts your growth."

Nola gave her a contemptuous smile. "MOCA stands for Museum of Contemporary Art."

"Oh." Maggie blushed.

Kaitlyn frowned. Why did Nola have to say it like that? Maggie had only been trying to be nice.

"My class went to an Andy Warhol exhibit there," Nola went on. "He was this really famous artist from the sixties," she added, looking at Liesel.

"I *know* who Andy Warhol is," Liesel snapped. She glanced across the table at Kaitlyn with a look that said, *Who does this girl think she is?*

Kaitlyn gave a miniscule shrug in reply.

"Anyway," Maggie said quickly, "Kaitlyn is an amazing babysitter. You should see her at the elementary school. She's practically a celebrity over there."

"Yeah." Kaitlyn laughed. "The Wiggles have got nothing on me."

To Kaitlyn's surprise, Nola's face lit up. "Really? I babysit, too!"

"Oh yeah?" Kaitlyn looked at her with new interest. She didn't think Nola could be a very good babysitter. She looked like she didn't like to get messy.

"I just love little kids," Nola gushed.

Kaitlyn nodded. "Yeah, the kids are cute. And," she added, giving Liesel a meaningful look, "it's a good way to *save* money."

Liesel rolled her eyes. "I'm working on it!"

Nola glanced from one to the other, looking confused.

"We're saving up for a trip to Wonder World," Maggie explained.

"What's Wonder World?" Nola asked.

The three girls stared at her. "You've never heard of Wonder World?" Kaitlyn asked, aghast.

"Wow, you really *aren't* from around here," said Liesel. "Wonder World is . . ."

"'Five acres of pure fun!'" Kaitlyn and Maggie chimed in, quoting from the TV commercial.

"No, really," Liesel said, "it's this huge amusement park about three hours away from here. It's got the biggest roller coaster in ten states!"

"Anyway, we've been wanting to go *forever*," said Maggie.

"At least since fifth grade," said Kaitlyn. "And my mom finally agreed to take us. Only we have to save up the money." She nudged Liesel with her foot.

"I'm working on it!" Liesel repeated. "Don't worry, I have lots of ideas for saving money."

"Name one," Kaitlyn demanded.

"Well, see these quarters?" Liesel held up two coins. "I'm *not* going to spend them on a soda. Instead, I'm going to put them in my pocket and *save* them."

"That's not enough for a soda, anyway," Kaitlyn pointed out.

"All the more reason to save them," Liesel said. She tucked the quarters into the front pocket of her jeans.

"Well, it's a start," Kaitlyn allowed.

Liesel crumpled up her lunch bag and tossed it into a trash can. Then she turned to Kaitlyn and blinked innocently. "Can I borrow some money for a Coke?"

"Liesel!"

"Pretty please, with whipped cream and a cherry on top?"

"I'm serious!" Kaitlyn said. But she was laughing. So was Maggie. Nola smiled uncertainly.

With a pointed sigh, Kaitlyn reached into her pocket and took out some change.

"*Thank you*, Kaitlyn," Liesel singsonged. She took the quarters and skipped over to the vending machine.

"So," said Maggie, turning back to Nola, "what amusement parks do you have in L.A.?"

"Well," Nola began, "I don't really —"

She was interrupted by an electronic jingling. Kaitlyn quickly pulled her cell phone from her pocket and turned off the ringer before the lunchroom monitor could hear it.

"Nice phone," Nola said.

Kaitlyn smiled. The cell phone had been her first major purchase with her babysitting money. She was the only one of her friends who had one.

"I used to have the same one, until I upgraded." Nola whipped out her cell phone. It was the same brand as Kaitlyn's, but a newer model. She flipped it open and showed Kaitlyn the picture on the screen. "Look, that's my dog. Isn't he cute?"

There was something about the proud tilt of

Nola's chin that Kaitlyn didn't like. "Excuse me," she said. "I need to get this."

As the other girls continued their conversation, Kaitlyn turned her body slightly away and answered the phone. "Hello?"

"Kaitlyn! Thank goodness you picked up." It was Mrs. Bailey, one of her best customers. "I'm so glad I reached you. We have a bit of a babysitting emergency. Mr. Bailey got invited to dinner with the partners at his firm — he's up for a promotion, you know — and we really need a sitter tonight."

"Did you say *tonight*?" Kaitlyn put her hand over her free ear to try to block out noise from the cafeteria. "I'm really sorry, Mrs. Bailey, but I'm busy tonight."

"Oh no. Are you sure? We only need you for a few hours — maybe from five to eight? You know, Kaitlyn, you're our favorite sitter."

"Thanks, Mrs. Bailey, but —"

"This is very important to us. I'll pay you *double* your normal price."

"Wow. I really wish I could. I'm sorry, Mrs. Bailey." Kaitlyn really *was* sorry. Double her normal price was a lot of money.

"Oh. Well, thanks, anyway, Kaitlyn." Mrs. Bailey sounded positively crushed.

"I hope you find someone," said Kaitlyn. "Bye, Mrs. Bailey."

Kaitlyn hung up and turned back to her friends. Liesel had returned with her soda, and now she and Nola were debating whether loop-de-loop roller coasters were scarier than regular up-and-down roller coasters.

Kaitlyn only half listened. She was still thinking about the offer Mrs. Bailey had just made. *Double* her normal price. That would mean *twice* as much money for Wonder World.

Kaitlyn was certain Maggie would come through with the money for their trip. Even though Maggie didn't have a job like Kaitlyn's, she was saving all her allowance and birthday money.

It was Liesel Kaitlyn was worried about. As far as she knew, Liesel had now saved a grand total of fifty cents, and the trip was only a few months away. At this rate, there was no way she would have enough saved in time. But they couldn't go without Liesel. It wouldn't be the same.

Liesel might not have any way to earn money, Kaitlyn thought. *But I do.*

Kaitlyn began to calculate. She could help pay for Liesel's trip, at least until Liesel could pay her back. It would mean that she'd have to save twice as much. So that's what she would do — starting today.

There was just one problem: the Knopfskys. She was already scheduled to babysit for them that afternoon. Kaitlyn didn't like to think about canceling at the last minute. She prided herself on being reliable.

I'll only do it this one time, she told herself. *We need the money, and this deal is just too good to pass up.*

She started to form her plan. She'd call the Knopfskys and tell them . . . tell them what?

"I'm sick," Kaitlyn murmured.

"You're sick?" Maggie's voice jolted her out of her thoughts. "Really? What's wrong?"

Kaitlyn blinked. Maggie, Liesel, and Nola were all staring at her.

"No, no." Kaitlyn shook her head. "Sorry. I was just thinking aloud."

"Well, come on, then," said Maggie. "The bell just rang."

Kaitlyn stood up from the table. "You guys go ahead. I have to make a phone call."

"I'll wait for you," said Liesel.

"No, really. Go ahead," Kaitlyn said. "I'm right behind you."

Kaitlyn slipped out the side door of the cafeteria. It was a gray, drizzly March day, the kind that made Kaitlyn think spring would never come. The rain had whittled the snow in the school yard down to sad, wet lumps.

She found the Knopfskys' number in her phone and dialed. Kaitlyn licked her lips, feeling nervous. She had never lied to a customer before.

"Hello, Mrs. Knopfsky? It's Kaitlyn," she said. Her voice cracked a little. She hoped that was a good thing. Maybe it would make her sound sicker.

"Hi, Kaitlyn," said Mrs. Knopfsky. "How are you? The kids are looking forward to seeing you this afternoon."

"Well, that's the thing. I'm really sorry, but . . ." Kaitlyn took a deep breath. "I don't think I can make it. I'm not feeling so good. I think I'm coming down with something."

"That's too bad." Mrs. Knopfsky sounded truly concerned. "What do you think it is?"

"Uh . . . I don't know," Kaitlyn mumbled. *Think of something!* she told herself. "I'm super tired. And I have this really, really sore throat." She tried to make her voice sound hoarse, like it was painful to talk.

15

"Oh no! You certainly should stay home. Do you know anyone else who could sit on short notice?"

Kaitlyn wished she'd thought of that. Instead of canceling, she should have asked Liesel or Maggie to take the job for her. But Maggie had volleyball practice after school, and Liesel claimed she hated to babysit.

"No, I'm sorry. I don't," Kaitlyn said.

"Well, we'll figure something out. Thank you for calling. And feel better." Mrs. Knopfsky hung up.

Kaitlyn leaned against the outside wall of the cafeteria and took a deep breath. Lying felt worse than she'd thought it would — especially since Mrs. Knopfsky had been so nice. But the worst was over. She only had one more call to make.

She scrolled back through her recent calls and dialed.

"Hello, Mrs. Bailey? It's Kaitlyn Sweeney. Guess what! It looks like I can sit for you after all!"

Chapter Two

Kaitlyn sighed and glanced at the DVD player. The digital clock read 9:26. The Baileys were almost an hour and a half late getting home.

She got up from the sofa. In her socks, she quietly crept down the hall to check on Rosie. The little girl was asleep in her bed, hands up alongside her ears, her lips parted in a tiny *O*. Kaitlyn tucked the blanket more tightly around her. She tiptoed out of the room, leaving the door slightly ajar.

Back in the living room, she flopped down on the sofa. With a jingle of dog tags, the Baileys' dachshund, Brutus, hopped up next to her. Kaitlyn patted his head. Brutus was one of the main reasons she liked sitting for the Baileys. She had always wanted a dog, but her father was allergic.

Kaitlyn picked up the television remote and began to flip through channels. Cop show. TV movie. Wrestling. News. Boring. Boring. Boring. Boring.

Kaitlyn glanced at the clock again. 9:29.

Each minute is more money, she reminded herself.

Still, she felt antsy. Even if the Baileys walked in the door that second, it would be too late to go over to Maggie's house. She'd missed yet another night with her friends. It seemed like she'd missed a lot of them lately.

Not that she was complaining. After all, how many other seventh graders had jobs? And she had to admit, she loved it when she went to the park or the grocery store and little kids screamed her name like she was some kind of celebrity.

No, she told herself, babysitting was definitely a good thing. She just sometimes wished she could spend as much time with her friends as she used to.

She continued to channel surf until she found a movie. It was one she'd seen before and she thought it was kind of dumb. But the main actor was cute. He reminded her a little of Topher.

Topher. Kaitlyn cringed, recalling their encounter earlier that day. Had he really not noticed that mouthful of mulched turkey sandwich she'd shown him, or was he just too nice to say anything?

Do I like Topher? Kaitlyn wondered, remembering her conversation with Liesel and Maggie at lunch. There was no question that he was crush-worthy. But Topher barely seemed to notice Kaitlyn. They hadn't said more than about three different words all year. Kaitlyn had been counting. Mostly it had been "hey," though there was the occasional "hi," and once, when Topher was passing back a stack of papers in Spanish class, "here." Kaitlyn was no expert, but you didn't need to be a genius to figure out that "hey" plus "hi" plus "here" did not add up to the language of love.

The way Kaitlyn saw it, if she liked Topher and Topher didn't even register her existence, then she was in a losing situation. And Kaitlyn preferred winning situations. In fact, she just preferred winning.

So the only conclusion she could possibly draw was that she didn't like Topher.

He sure is cute, though, Kaitlyn thought with a sigh. She remembered the way he had smiled at her in the cafeteria.

A key scraped in the lock, and the front door opened. Kaitlyn leaped up from the sofa.

"We're home!" Mrs. Bailey said in a loud whisper, coming into the room.

Kaitlyn put a hand to her cheek. She was blushing as if Topher had actually been there. Not that she would ever have a boy over. That was the number one rule of babysitting: no boys in the house.

"I'm sorry we're so late," Mr. Bailey told Kaitlyn as Mrs. Bailey went to check on Rosie. "The dinner lasted much longer than we expected."

"It's okay," said Kaitlyn.

Mrs. Bailey came back into the room, looking satisfied. "Sound asleep," she said.

Kaitlyn nodded. "I heated up that lasagna for her dinner, and then we played with the blocks for a while and I read her *Goodnight Moon.* She went to bed about seven-thirty. Oh, and Rosie's grandmother called. I left the message on the notepad next to the phone."

Kaitlyn had discovered that parents wanted to know every detail, down to which storybooks she read their kids at bedtime. So she always gave a full report. She considered it her trademark.

"You're the best, Kaitlyn," said Mr. Bailey.

Kaitlyn smiled.

Mrs. Bailey took her wallet out of her purse and plucked several bills from inside. "Here you go," she said, handing them to Kaitlyn. "We really appreciate you coming on such short notice."

"It's my pleasure," Kaitlyn said. She folded the money and put it in her pocket. The wad of bills made a lump in her jeans.

"I'll give you a lift," Mrs. Bailey said. "Are you still going to your friend's house?"

Kaitlyn glanced at the DVD clock. 9:59. Much too late to go over to Maggie's.

"That's okay, Mrs. Bailey," she said. "You can just take me home."

Chapter Three

Saturday morning, Kaitlyn was talking to Maggie on her cell and eating cereal straight out of the box, when her call waiting beeped.

"Hold on, Maggie," said Kaitlyn, "there's another call coming in." She switched to the other line.

"Kaitlyn?" said a man's voice.

"Speaking."

"Kaitlyn, hi. It's Mr. Brown."

"Hi, Mr. Brown!" Kaitlyn chirped. The Browns were the people she was sitting for that night. Kaitlyn liked sitting for the Browns. Their kids were pretty well behaved, not to mention they had premium cable and good snacks.

"We just wanted to check in and see how you're feeling," Mr. Brown said.

"I feel fine," Kaitlyn said.

"Really? We saw the Knopfskys last night and they told us how sick you were."

Dang! Kaitlyn had forgotten that the Knopfskys and the Browns were best friends. "Oh, I'm feeling much better," she said hoarsely, trying to sound as if she was recovering from a cold. "Don't worry. I'll be there at six o'clock sharp."

"Oh no, no!" Mr. Brown said quickly. "Don't worry about us. We've already found another sitter."

Double dang! "I don't mind. I really do feel better."

"You need to stay home and get lots of rest. It takes a while to shake this sort of thing."

"If you're sure . . ." Kaitlyn said weakly.

"Sure as sure can be. Feel better, Kaitlyn."

"Okay, well, thanks, Mr. Brown."

Kaitlyn could've kicked herself. Her plan for doubling her pay had just backfired. She'd told a big fat lie, and for what? Now she was just breaking even.

As she got off the phone, it occurred to her to wonder who was sitting for the Browns. But before she could ask, Mr. Brown had hung up.

Later that afternoon, Kaitlyn rode her bike through the slushy streets to Liesel's house. Even though it was light out, the streetlights were starting to come on. Kaitlyn pedaled faster. She wasn't supposed to be riding after dark.

At the end of her road, she turned left onto Lakeside Drive. Marshfield Lake, the suburb Kaitlyn and her friends lived in, was built around a man-made lake. Kaitlyn lived on one side of the lake, Liesel lived on the other, and Maggie lived in between. Kaitlyn had always thought Marshfield Lake was a funny name. It sounded like three different places: marsh, field, lake. But there were no marshes or fields in Marshfield Lake. "Marshfield" came from Henry Marshfield, the developer who'd built most of the houses in their town. He had died before Kaitlyn was born, but his son and his son's family lived in a big mansion on a hill overlooking the lake.

Kaitlyn had never met the Marshfields, but she'd seen them riding through town in a chauffeured Mercedes-Benz. She'd heard they had two kids, but Kaitlyn didn't know how old the kids were. They had a live-in nanny, so they didn't need a babysitter.

As Kaitlyn coasted up the alley that led to the back of Liesel's house, Liesel came darting out the door. She was wearing galoshes and an extra-large sweatshirt over a pair of leggings.

"You can't come in this way," Liesel said, heading her off. "The painting is drying in the kitchen. You'll have to go around to the front of the house."

For weeks, Liesel had been working on her painting for the youth art show. She wouldn't let anyone see it, not even her mother. Everyone was on strict instructions to stay out of the kitchen when Liesel was working.

Kaitlyn parked her bike at the back of the house, then trudged through the melting snow around to the front door.

Liesel met her there. "Maggie's up in my room," she said. "I'll bring some drinks up. The painting will be dry in a while, and then I can move it."

As Liesel headed off to the kitchen, Kaitlyn climbed the stairs to Liesel's room. Most of the houses in Marshfield Lake had the same floor plan, give or take a few rooms. It was possible to go into a total stranger's house and still know exactly where their bathroom and kitchen and coat closet were. Liesel's room was in the same place as Kaitlyn's room was in her house — on the southwest-facing side.

The similarity ended at the door, however. Whereas Kaitlyn had the same peach-colored walls and matching floral bedspread she'd had since first grade, Liesel's walls were covered with her sketches and paintings. Kaitlyn couldn't remember what Liesel's bedspread looked like, because the bed was always buried under clothes.

"Look out! Babysitter on the loose!" Maggie cried as Kaitlyn walked through the door. "There's no telling what this diaper-changing daredevil might do on her night off."

Kaitlyn grinned. Maggie was curled up in an overstuffed chair. Her long hair framed her face like a curtain.

Kaitlyn moved a pile of clothes and sat down on the bed. "You know, I was bummed about it before, but now I'm actually kind of glad my babysitting job got canceled. I'm psyched to have a night just to hang out." She didn't bother to go into the whole story of how she'd tried to double her money for Liesel's sake. Somehow she didn't think Maggie would approve.

"Speaking of babysitting, look what I found at the supermarket." Maggie reached into her back pocket and pulled out a folded square of bright yellow paper. She handed it to Kaitlyn.

Kaitlyn unfolded it. "'Need a babysitter?'" she read. "'Call Nola for the best in professional babysitting! The latest techniques in child care. Excellent references. Educational games and organic snacks provided.' And here's her number. Is this . . . ?"

Maggie nodded. "The new girl. It must be. I mean, how many people are named Nola?"

Kaitlyn studied the flyer. "She's charging a dollar less than me. And what does 'the latest techniques in child care' mean?"

"I don't know. But I'm sure she's got nothing on you," said Maggie. "Everyone knows you're the best babysitter in town."

"Yeah," said Kaitlyn. Still, she felt a spark of annoyance. Educational games? Organic snacks? Whatever.

Kaitlyn crumpled up the flyer and threw it in the trash.

"Dinner is served," Liesel said from the doorway. She held up three cans of root beer. "Just kidding," she added, seeing Maggie's horrified look. She tossed a can to Maggie and came to sit next to Kaitlyn on the bed.

Maggie tapped her fingernails on the top of the can to settle the bubbles. "So what do you guys want to do tonight?"

"We could play Monopoly," Kaitlyn suggested.

"No!" Maggie and Liesel shouted.

"It was just a suggestion," Kaitlyn said defensively. She loved Monopoly, but she could never get her friends to play with her, just because *one time* she'd thrown the board out the window when she was losing. It was totally unfair. For Pete's sake, that had been over a year ago!

"We could order pizza," Maggie said.

"Pizza!" Kaitlyn seconded.

Liesel picked up her phone. "Pepperoni?"

"With olives," said Kaitlyn.

"With mushrooms," said Maggie.

"With olives and mushrooms," said Kaitlyn.

Liesel made a face. She dialed the number of the pizza place. "Hi, a large pizza for delivery? Pepperoni, with olives and mushrooms *on half.*" She gave them her address and phone number and hung up.

"How are you going to keep up your strength for the art show if you don't eat your vegetables?" Kaitlyn teased.

"Root beer *is* a vegetable," Liesel replied. "It's a root."

"I can't wait for the show," Maggie gushed. "What are you going to wear, Liesel? You have to look super glamorous."

Liesel shrugged. "No, I don't. I'm an artist, not a fashion model."

"But it's your big debut!" Maggie protested.

"So I'll look like an artist. This is what artists look like." Liesel gestured toward her paint-splattered sweatshirt.

"Come on. Everyone likes to look good." Kaitlyn got up and went over to the closet. "There's got to be something in here." She yanked a silky dress off a hanger. "What about this?"

Liesel snorted. "That's a bathrobe."

Kaitlyn took a closer look. "Oh yeah. It's kind of pretty, though." She slipped it over her sweater and jeans and twirled around. "Maybe people will think it's a kimono."

"Try again," said Maggie.

Kaitlyn plunged her hands back into the closet. She came up with a denim dress that snapped up the front.

"That fit great . . . in fifth grade," said Liesel.

Kaitlyn studied it. "How come you never wore it in fifth grade?"

"I did once, remember? I was climbing on the jungle gym at recess and that jerk Branson Farley made fun of my skinny legs."

"Ohhhhh," Kaitlyn and Maggie said, remembering. Kaitlyn put the dress back into the closet.

She flipped through the rest of the clothes on the hangers. "Flannel, flannel, hoodie, thermal, down vest, thermal . . . oh, and these." She held up a pair of jeans that had been patched in so many places there was hardly any denim left.

"I've been looking for those!" Liesel cried. "I wonder how they got in the closet?"

Kaitlyn shut the closet door. "Well, you may have to go in that sweatshirt after all. You definitely do not have any fancy clothes."

"What about your mom?" Maggie asked. "My mom has all these old dresses in the back of her closet, stuff that doesn't fit her anymore. She never throws away anything."

Liesel thought for a moment. "There's some old stuff in the closet of the wreck room."

"Let's check it out," Kaitlyn said, setting down her soda.

The wreck room was just down the hall from Liesel's room. It was called that because it always looked like a hurricane had recently been through. Broken furniture competed for space with empty bottles, egg cartons, jars of old paintbrushes, piles of magazines, short-circuited appliances, dusty baskets of plastic fruit, and anything else that Liesel and her mother couldn't bring themselves to throw away.

Kaitlyn opened the closet door. "How do you find anything in here?" she asked.

"We don't," said Liesel.

Kaitlyn pushed aside some musty old coats and a vacuum cleaner that looked like it had sucked its last breath in about 1970. She moved an old tennis racket and almost got clobbered by a tower of falling shoe boxes. At the back she found a black hanging bag.

"What's this?" she asked. Liesel shrugged.

Kaitlyn took the bag out of the closet. She cleared a space on the floor to lay it down and unzipped it.

"Wow!" said Maggie.

Inside was a sleek black sleeveless dress. Kaitlyn turned it over. A row of pearl buttons ran up the back.

Maggie ran her fingers over the material. "It feels like velvet!"

Liesel stared at the dress. "Wait a second," she said. She left the room and returned a moment later carrying a photograph.

"Look," she said. The photograph was of Liesel's mother, looking much younger than Kaitlyn had ever seen her. She was standing next to a large abstract painting.

"It's my mom at her first art show," Liesel explained.

"She's wearing the same dress!" said Maggie.

Liesel nodded. "I always liked this picture."

"Now you *have* to wear it!" said Kaitlyn. "It'll be like tradition."

"Try it on," Maggie urged.

Liesel pulled off her sweatshirt and slipped the dress over her head. Maggie helped her with the buttons in the back.

"Ooh!" Maggie breathed. "You look a-MA-zing."

Kaitlyn had to agree. Even with her leggings and sloppy ponytail, Liesel looked very elegant in the dress.

Liesel turned to an old mirror leaning up against one wall and studied herself. "It's too big around the middle."

"You can belt it or something," Maggie suggested.

"Don't you like it?" Kaitlyn asked Liesel.

Liesel broke into a smile. "It totally rocks."

"Yeah!" Maggie cheered.

"You're going to be awesome, Liesel," Kaitlyn said.

Liesel put her arms around her friends' shoulders. "You guys promise you'll be there, right?"

"Are you kidding?" Maggie cried.

"Cross my heart and hope to die," Kaitlyn said.

Chapter Four

The following Wednesday, Kaitlyn and Liesel were in their usual lunch spot, at the yellow table near the vending machines. It was another wet March day. The smell of rain blew in through an open side door, mingling with the lunchroom odors of pizza, french fry grease, and disinfectant.

"It's weird," Kaitlyn said, checking her messages for the fourth time that day.

"What's weird?" asked Liesel.

"It's the middle of the week, and I haven't gotten any calls to babysit this weekend," Kaitlyn said.

"Bummer," Liesel said. She didn't sound like she meant it.

"Yeah, but usually *somebody* has called me by now," Kaitlyn told her.

"Well, probably someone will call soon," Liesel said. She pulled a sandwich wrapped in waxed paper out of a paper lunch sack. "Where's Maggie?"

"Dunno. She said she'd be late. Track meeting or — what *is* that?" Kaitlyn stopped and stared. Centered on the waxed paper in front of Liesel was a stack of soggy bread slices stuck together with red, purple, and white goop.

"Strawberry jam, grape jelly, and Marshmallow Fluff," Liesel said proudly. "It's my latest masterpiece. I call it 'Lunch.'"

"I call it 'gross.'" Kaitlyn watched her take a bite. "You know, there's, like, no nutritional value in that whatsoever."

"Whatever, Miss Four Food Groups. It tastes good," said Liesel. She took another bite. A blob of jam oozed out the side of the sandwich and dropped onto the yellow tabletop.

"It makes my teeth hurt just looking at you," Kaitlyn said. She rummaged in her lunch sack and came up with a bag of carrot sticks. She pushed them toward her friend. "Feel free to help yourself," she said, even though she knew Liesel wouldn't.

To her surprise, Liesel reached for a carrot stick. But as her fingers touched the vegetable, she let out a shriek. "I'm melting! I'm mel-l-l-l-lting!"

Liesel slid down in her seat, doing her best Wicked Witch of the West imitation.

Kaitlyn laughed. She grabbed a carrot stick and pointed it at Liesel. "Do what I say, or you'll get the carrot," she threatened in a gangsterlike voice.

"No, not the carrot! Anything but the carrot!" Liesel widened her eyes in mock horror as Kaitlyn slowly moved the carrot closer and closer. Kaitlyn paused, with the carrot hovering right in front of Liesel's face. Then she tapped her on the nose. Liesel collapsed.

Kaitlyn cracked up. For a moment, Liesel remained slumped in her chair, eyes rolled back and tongue hanging out to show how devastated she was by her near-vegetable experience.

As Liesel straightened up, she glanced at someone behind Kaitlyn's back and raised an eyebrow. Kaitlyn turned to look. The new girl, Nola, was sitting by herself at the next table, watching them. As soon as Kaitlyn caught her eye, Nola looked down at her lunch tray.

"Do you think we should ask her to sit with us?" Kaitlyn asked Liesel.

Liesel frowned. "She seems kind of full of herself, don't you think?"

"Kind of. But Maggie likes her."

"Maggie likes everyone," Liesel pointed out. "Remember Nina the nosepicker?"

"How could I forget?" said Kaitlyn. Nina had been the new girl in fourth grade.

"Maggie was nice to her, too, and then she wouldn't leave us alone," said Liesel. "She was always hanging around, trying to get us to trade our sandwiches for her boogery ones."

"I remember," Kaitlyn said with a shudder.

"And there was that time she wrote a mean note to me and said it was from you, so you would stop being my friend."

"That I *don't* remember," Kaitlyn said. But she knew it must have happened. When someone had done her wrong, Liesel never forgot it.

"Point being," said Liesel, "that new girl might seem normal, but you never know who's going to turn out to be a nosepicker."

"I guess you're right," said Kaitlyn. She glanced once more at Nola. The new girl was staring down at her plate, tentatively prodding a piece of school-lunch lasagna with her fork.

Suddenly, Kaitlyn felt kind of sorry for Nola. Kaitlyn had known her best friends since kindergarten. She took it for granted that they would always be there. She had no idea what it would feel like to be at a new school, without knowing anyone at all.

She doesn't look *like a nosepicker,* Kaitlyn thought. *But Liesel is right, you never can tell.*

With a shrug, she turned back to her lunch.

Chapter Five

By Thursday, Kaitlyn was sure something was up. The weekend was one day away, and she still hadn't received a single call to babysit.

Had the Knopfskys somehow found out that she'd lied? Kaitlyn wondered as she sat waiting for Spanish class to begin. Had they called other parents, who'd called other parents, until everyone in town thought Kaitlyn Sweeney was a big fat liar? Just thinking about that made Kaitlyn feel sick to her stomach.

The classroom was full of noise as other kids took their seats. At the front of the room, Señora Ramos was writing the daily challenge word on the board. Every day, she wrote a new Spanish word or phrase. Whoever could provide the English translation first without using a dictionary got a bonus point, and the person with the most bonus points at the end of the school year would win a gift certificate to a local Mexican restaurant. So far, Kaitlyn was ahead, but Topher was a close second.

Señora Ramos had barely written the last letter, when Kaitlyn raised her hand. *"En boca cerrada no entran moscas,"* Kaitlyn read from the board. "It means 'Flies don't enter a closed mouth.'"

"In other words?" said Señora Ramos.

"Shut your mouth," Kaitlyn interpreted.

"Muy bien," said Señora Ramos, giving a meaningful look to two girls who were still chatting. The girls abruptly stopped talking.

Kaitlyn glanced down at her desk and smiled.

Señora Ramos began to describe the dialogue exercise they were going to do in class that day. As Kaitlyn opened her notebook, she heard someone in front of her say, "How did you know that?"

Kaitlyn looked up. Topher had swiveled around in his seat and was staring at her. "I'm sure it's not in our Spanish book," he said. "Are you getting the answers from someone, or something?"

Kaitlyn's mouth fell open. She didn't know whether to be amazed that Topher was talking to her or angry that he had just accused her of cheating. "No, I'm not getting the answers," she said. "We learned all those words in class." Then she sassily added, hardly believing her nerve, "You just have to be smart enough to put them all together."

For a second, Topher looked annoyed. Then his expression softened. "Sorry," he said. "I didn't mean to sound like a jerk. It's just that I was surprised. I've flipped through most of the textbook, and I'm pretty sure I didn't see that phrase."

"Aha," Kaitlyn said. "Reading ahead in the book — so *that's* how you've been getting all those challenge words."

"Well" — Topher gave her a lopsided smile — "aren't you?"

Kaitlyn couldn't help smiling back. "Yup," she admitted.

"So . . ." Topher leaned a bit closer. "Are you going to tell me your secret or what?"

Kaitlyn had never been this close to his face before. She noticed his blue-green irises had little flecks of gray. "I don't know," she told him, trying to sound cool. "It's pretty embarrassing."

"Try me," said Topher.

"I watch Spanish soap operas and write down words I don't know," Kaitlyn confessed. "There's this one character who is always telling her husband to keep his mouth shut. *En boca cerrada no entran moscas,*" she repeated, wagging her finger like the woman on the show.

Topher laughed. "Wow, you're serious. You must really want that gift certificate."

"What can I say?" Kaitlyn replied with a shrug, though her heart was racing. "I like Mexican food."

"Linda. Jose." Señora Ramos suddenly loomed over them.

Kaitlyn and Topher glanced up guiltily. Linda and Jose were their Spanish-class names.

"Why don't I hear you speaking Spanish?" Señora Ramos asked with a frown.

Suddenly Kaitlyn realized that all the other students in the class were talking to each other in Spanish. On the board, the challenge phrase had been replaced by a list of words they were supposed to be using in their dialogue exercise.

"Perdóname," said Topher.

"That's better," said Señora Ramos. She moved on down the row.

"So," Kaitlyn said to Topher with a sly smile. She pointed to the board. "I'll bet you can't use all those words in one sentence."

Topher grinned. "Watch me," he said.

Later that night, Kaitlyn stood at the kitchen sink, washing the dinner dishes. Her father stood next to her, drying. Kaitlyn's mother and six-year-old sister, Lily, sat at the kitchen table, working on Lily's homework.

Kaitlyn couldn't stop thinking about her conversation with Topher. She couldn't believe that in just one class, they'd gone from being on a three-word basis to, well, too many words to count. She laughed, remembering how Topher had tried to cram all those vocab words into one long, ridiculous sentence.

"What's so funny?" her dad asked.

"Nothing," Kaitlyn said. "I was just thinking about Spanish."

The phone rang. Kaitlyn wiped her soapy hands on a dish towel and answered it.

"Kaitlyn!" said a chipper voice. "It's Mrs. Arnold."

"Hi, Mrs. Arnold. Let me get my mom." Mrs. Arnold was one of her mother's best friends.

"Actually, Kaitlyn, I was hoping to catch you. We're looking for a sitter tomorrow night. Are you free?"

Normally Kaitlyn would have said no. Not that she had anything against Mrs. Arnold. She was a perfectly nice person, and her husband, Mr. Arnold, was nice, too. The problem was their two-year-old son, Troy. Troy was not nice. Troy was an absolute terror. The first — and last — time Kaitlyn ever sat for him she had nicknamed him "the Monster."

If Kaitlyn had been thinking, she would have politely explained that she was busy for the next five or ten years and gotten off the phone as soon as possible. But Kaitlyn wasn't thinking at the moment. Or rather, she was thinking about Topher.

Before she knew what she was doing, Kaitlyn heard herself say, "Sure, Mrs. Arnold. That sounds great."

As she got off the phone, Kaitlyn slapped herself on the forehead. She'd just agreed to babysit the most obnoxious kid in town!

Chapter Six

On Friday, Kaitlyn decided to bring her Spanish book with her to social studies class. It was such a good idea she wondered why she hadn't thought of it before.

"This way," she explained to Maggie as they walked out of class together, "I don't have to go back to my locker between classes. Instead, I can go past *Topher's* locker, and it'll look like I'm just on my way to Spanish class."

"You *are* on your way to Spanish class," Maggie reminded her.

"Right," said Kaitlyn. "And Topher will be on his way to class, too, so maybe we'll walk together."

"I thought you didn't like him," Maggie said with a smile.

"Well, I'm not sure. I might," Kaitlyn admitted.

"What changed?"

Kaitlyn shrugged. "I don't know. We speak the same language."

She paused at the end of the corridor. "How do I look?" She fluffed the ends of her hair. She was wearing her favorite shirt, the one that brought out the green in her eyes.

"You look great," said Maggie.

"Thanks."

Kaitlyn started off down the corridor, cradling her stack of books in her arms. Fortunately, the hall wasn't too crowded. She would be able to see Topher's locker from a distance, so she could time their "chance" meeting.

There he was, alone at his locker, just like she'd hoped he would be.

Ooh! He was so cute! She quickened her pace.

Soon Kaitlyn was only a few feet away. She was about to begin her leisurely stroll through Topher's line of vision when suddenly, from out of nowhere, a girl swooped in right under her nose.

It was Nola.

As Kaitlyn watched, Nola began to talk to Topher. From the way Nola was standing, leaning in close to him, Kaitlyn could tell she didn't want anyone else to hear what they were saying. Kaitlyn couldn't guess what they were talking about, but it was pretty obvious that they had more than a three-word relationship.

Topher handed Nola a folded-up sheet of paper. Nola gave a little nod, like she was agreeing to something. Then she turned and walked away.

Kaitlyn stared after her, confused. What had just happened? How did Nola know Topher? And what was on that folded-up piece of paper?

Suddenly Kaitlyn realized that she was still standing in the middle of the hallway. Kids were passing on her left and right. She shook herself and continued on to class.

In Spanish class, Kaitlyn waited for Topher to turn around, but he never did. For the rest of the day, Kaitlyn's thoughts swirled around Topher and Nola. They had acted so secretive. But Nola had been at school for only a week. What kind of secret could she possibly have with Topher? Unless . . .

Could Nola *like* Topher?

Worse thought: Could Topher like *Nola*?

By the time Kaitlyn got home from school that day, she felt exhausted from thinking about it.

Kaitlyn's mother was sitting at the kitchen table, talking on the phone. Mrs. Sweeney was head of the Parent-Teacher Association at Lily's school, and she spent a lot of time talking to other parents. She called it "networking." Kaitlyn called it "gossiping."

Kaitlyn took a carton of milk out of the fridge, poured herself a glass, and got a stack of sandwich cookies from a jar on the counter. She carried her snack over to the table. She could hear the television on in the den where her little sister was watching *Sesame Street*.

Mrs. Sweeney finished her conversation and hung up. "Hi, sweetie," she said to Kaitlyn. "How was school?"

"Fine," Kaitlyn replied automatically.

"Are you babysitting tonight, honey? I was just talking to the Nichols down the street. They need a sitter, if you're free."

"I *wish* I were free," Kaitlyn groaned. "But I already said I'd sit for the Monster."

Her mother's forehead wrinkled. "Who?"

Oops. Kaitlyn had never told her mother her nickname for Mrs. Arnold's kid. "Troy Arnold," she said quickly.

"Oh?" Mrs. Sweeney looked surprised. "I thought you said you'd never sit for them again."

Kaitlyn rolled her eyes. "Momentary lapse of reason." Kaitlyn wished she could cancel on the

Arnolds and take the job with the Nichols, who had a sweet little six-month-old. But she'd learned her lesson the week before.

"Well, in that case, the Nichols want to know if you've heard of another sitter — someone named Nola?"

Kaitlyn choked on her cookie. She grabbed her glass of milk and took a huge gulp.

"They say they've been hearing great things about her," Mrs. Sweeney went on, apparently not noticing that her daughter had almost inhaled an entire Oreo. "She has all these wonderful ways of entertaining kids. . . . Are you all right, honey?"

"Just went down the wrong pipe," Kaitlyn said hoarsely. She wiped her watering eyes with the back of her hand.

"Don't eat so fast," her mother advised. "So, do you know this girl, Nola?"

"There's a new girl at school named Nola," Kaitlyn said cautiously. "I don't really know her, though. Um, what did the Nichols say about her?"

"Well, apparently she's done some sitting for the Browns and the Parkers and the Davises, and everyone was very happy with her."

The Browns and the Parkers and the Davises? Those were *her* customers!

Kaitlyn stood up from the table.

"What's wrong?" her mother asked.

"I have to go make some calls," Kaitlyn replied. "Can you give me a ride to the Arnolds' later?"

"Yes," Mrs. Sweeney replied, "but tell them they'll need to drive you home if they're going to be late."

"I will," Kaitlyn said, already halfway out the door.

Something weird is going on, she thought as she stormed up the stairs to her bedroom. *And I'm going to get to the bottom of it.*

Chapter Seven

"No," said Kaitlyn. "No, no, no, no, no."

She planted her hands on her hips. "Are you listening to me?"

The Monster gave her an innocent look. Without taking his gaze from her face, he wrapped his plump little hands around the refrigerator door handle and gave a defiant tug.

"No, Troy. You will not take one more thing out of this refrigerator," Kaitlyn said. She pushed the door closed and leaned against it.

The Monster screamed.

It was eight o'clock on Friday night. Kaitlyn had been at the Arnolds' for just under two hours. It felt like much, much longer.

Since the last time Kaitlyn had been there, the Monster had discovered a new hobby — "cooking."

Kaitlyn had naively assumed that "cooking" meant playing with pots and pans. She knew lots of little kids who liked to sit on the floor and bang on a pot with a spoon. While she'd searched the cupboards for suitable cookware, Troy had opened the refrigerator and emptied the entire vegetable bin onto the kitchen floor.

This, apparently, was what "cooking" meant.

As Kaitlyn had chased a runaway potato to the far corner of the room, Troy had gotten into the refrigerator again and spilled a whole jar of olives.

Now they were in a standoff. Kaitlyn folded her arms and pressed her full weight against the refrigerator door, while Troy, his footy pajamas soggy with olive juice, tugged at the handle and howled.

Kaitlyn glanced at the clock. Soon it would be too late to make the phone calls she desperately needed to make. That afternoon, she had called Liesel and Maggie to tell them about Nola stealing her customers. Liesel had been outraged, but Maggie thought there might be some other explanation. She had suggested that Kaitlyn call her clients and do some discreet snooping.

Which was exactly what Kaitlyn planned to do — if only she could get this demon in diapers to be quiet.

"Okay, okay!" Kaitlyn shouted above his wailing.

"Okay, Troy. Guess what? I'm going to let you 'cook.'"

The Monster's screams broke off as suddenly as if Kaitlyn had hit the PAUSE button. He looked at her with interest.

"That's right. We're going to cook. Only we're going to do it in the *bathtub*. Won't that be fun? So . . ." Kaitlyn opened the refrigerator door. "You get to pick *one* thing to play with. How about this nice carrot?" She waved a carrot in front of his face enticingly.

The Monster was no dummy. He dismissed the carrot with a curl of his lip and headed straight for a squeeze bottle of chocolate syrup.

Kaitlyn groaned inwardly.

She took the bottle of chocolate syrup in one hand, scooped up Troy with her other arm, and carried them both into the bathroom. Setting the toddler down in the tub, she stripped him down to his diaper and threw his soggy pajamas in the hamper.

"Okay, buddy boy," she said, handing him the bottle. "Cook something delicious."

The Monster squeezed the bottle and a stream of liquid chocolate hit the white porcelain side of the tub. He squealed with delight.

"Perfect," Kaitlyn said. She closed the shower curtain, which was made of clear vinyl, and settled atop the toilet. Now she could watch him without getting caught in the line of fire.

Kaitlyn took her cell phone out of her pocket. She decided to start with the Parkers. She'd sat for them just two weeks before, and everything had seemed fine then.

She dialed. Someone picked up on the second ring. "Hello?" It was a girl's voice.

"Hi," said Kaitlyn. "Could I speak to Mr. or Mrs. Parker?" She flinched as a stream of chocolate hit the shower curtain inches from her face.

"They're not in at the moment," the girl said pleasantly. "Can I take a message?"

"Who's this?" Kaitlyn asked.

"The babysitter."

Kaitlyn sucked in her breath. *The babysitter who?* she wanted to ask. "That's okay. I'll call back," she said. She hung up quickly.

Her heart was pounding. Had that been Nola's voice? She couldn't tell.

She checked on the Monster. He was sailing a rubber duck around in a puddle of chocolate syrup like some poor bird caught in an oil spill.

She decided to call someone else. She was afraid

the Browns would bring up last week, and she didn't want to lie again. So it would have to be the Davises. She dialed.

"Hello?" It was a little girl's voice.

"Is this Melissa?" Kaitlyn asked.

"Yeah."

"Hi, it's Kaitlyn, your babysitter."

"Hi, Kaitlyn," said Melissa.

"Is your mom or dad there?"

"Yeah." There was a pause. Kaitlyn could hear Melissa breathing.

"Can I talk to them?" Kaitlyn asked finally.

"Okay." Melissa put down the phone. Kaitlyn could hear her screaming, "Mo-o-o-om!" in another room.

A second later, Mrs. Davis picked up. "Hello?"

"Hi, Mrs. Davis, it's Kaitlyn. Kaitlyn Sweeney."

"Well, hello, Kaitlyn. What a surprise!"

Why a surprise? Kaitlyn wondered. "I was just calling to see how you were all doing. I haven't heard from you in a while."

"That's so sweet of you to call, especially considering how tired you must be. We're all doing fine. But how are *you* doing? Are you feeling any better?"

"I'm feeling fine," Kaitlyn said. She started to get a sinking feeling.

"We heard how sick you were. Mono is such a terrible illness. It takes some people *months* to recover."

"Mono!" Kaitlyn practically yelped. Who said she had mono?

"We heard you came down with it last week. It's just terrible."

Kaitlyn racked her brain. She was certain she hadn't told the Knopfskys she had mono. But what *had* she told them? Kaitlyn remembered saying that she was tired and had a sore throat. Had Mrs. Knopfsky somehow concluded that she had mono?

"I was going to ask you to babysit for us this week," Mrs. Davis was saying. "Luckily, we were able to find someone else."

"Who?" Kaitlyn blurted.

"A girl named Nola. She's new in town. She's a wonderful sitter. Melissa and Nick just adored her. She must go to your school. Do you know her?"

"No," Kaitlyn mumbled. "I haven't met her. Well, anyway, Mrs. Davis, I was just calling to say hi."

"Thank you for calling, Kaitlyn," Mrs. Davis replied. "I hope you feel better soon!"

Kaitlyn hung up the phone. "That little sneak!" she screeched, so loudly that the Monster dropped the bottle of chocolate.

Kaitlyn stood and began to pace. So, all the parents thought she had mono, and Nola was taking the chance to steal away her best customers. "For all I know, Nola started the rumor herself," Kaitlyn fumed. "I cannot *believe* I ever felt sorry for that girl!"

The Monster giggled. Clearly he thought the situation was funny.

Kaitlyn was tempted to call more parents. But it was almost eight-thirty and the bathtub looked like a chocolate volcano had erupted inside it. She still had to give the Monster a bath, put him to bed, and clean up the bathroom and the kitchen before the Arnolds got home.

And anyway, Kaitlyn told herself as she picked up a sponge, *I already found out all I need to know.*

Chapter Eight

Saturday morning, Kaitlyn, Liesel, and Maggie sat at the table in the Sweeneys' kitchen, drinking orange juice and eating easy-bake cinnamon rolls. First thing that morning, Kaitlyn had called an emergency meeting to discuss the Nola situation.

"So, I don't get it," Maggie said, when Kaitlyn had finished explaining. "Why do all these parents think you have mono?"

"I'll bet Nola started a rumor," Liesel said, before Kaitlyn could answer. "I'll bet she's trying to get you out of the picture, so she'll be the only baby-sitter in Marshfield Lake."

"Why would she do that?" asked Maggie. "There are lots of people who need babysitters."

"Who knows?" Kaitlyn said. "The point is, however

she's doing it, Nola is stealing my business, and I need to figure out a way to get it back."

"Why don't you just call all the parents and tell them you don't have mono?" Maggie suggested.

"Right. I'll just call all these people up and be like, 'Hi, it's Kaitlyn.'" Kaitlyn held a pretend phone to her ear. "'I was just calling to say that I don't have mono or any other contagious diseases.'"

"I guess that won't work," said Maggie.

"And, anyway, that's only part of the problem. Now they all know Nola. Last night, Mrs. Davis called her 'wonderful.' For all I know, every mom and dad in town already has her on speed dial."

"So you just have to remind them you're the better babysitter," said Maggie.

"Exactly." Kaitlyn nodded. "But the question is — how?"

Kaitlyn's sister, Lily, came into the kitchen. She was wearing a frilly dress and roller skates.

"Cinnamon rolls!" she said. She skated over to the table and reached for a roll.

Kaitlyn whipped the plate out of her reach. "Say 'please,' Lily."

Lily stuck out her lip. "Please," she sulked.

Kaitlyn handed her sister a roll. "Here's one. Now go away. We're having a private meeting."

"I want to meet, too," said Lily.

"Go watch TV," Kaitlyn said. She gave her sister a little nudge that sent her rolling toward the door.

"Well," said Maggie, getting back to business, "the way I see it, there are three things that need to happen. First, you need to get rid of the mono rumor. Second, you need to do some advertising to remind the parents that you're the best sitter around. And third, you need a hook."

"A hook?" said Kaitlyn.

"You know, like something that will make them realize what a great deal they're getting."

"Hmm," Kaitlyn said.

Her father wandered in, carrying an empty coffee mug. "Mmm," he said, "cinnamon rolls."

"Um, Dad?" Kaitlyn said as he reached for one. "We're kind of having a private meeting here."

"Private, eh?" her dad said. "A little seventh-grade espionage work? Don't worry, my lips are sealed."

Kaitlyn gave him a "please don't embarrass me" look.

"All right. I'm going," said Mr. Sweeney. He refilled his coffee cup and shuffled out of the kitchen.

"So, let's start with the rumor," said Maggie. "How do we get rid of it, when we don't even know who's heard it?"

"What about a counter rumor?" Liesel suggested. "We get someone to tell a few of the parents that Kaitlyn's *not* sick, and then they tell other parents — and *voilà*! Problem solved."

Maggie nodded. "Yeah. So you just need someone to start it off."

"But who?" Kaitlyn asked.

Kaitlyn's mother came into the kitchen. "I know, I know," Mrs. Sweeney said. "You're having a private meeting. I heard. I'm just coming to get the cordless." She took the phone off its cradle and walked back out of the kitchen.

Maggie looked at Kaitlyn.

"My mother?" Kaitlyn said. "No way!"

"But she already talks to all the parents, anyway," Maggie pointed out. "She doesn't even have to say you're sick. She could just let it slip how healthy you are, and you'll be back to babysitting in no time."

Kaitlyn thought about it. Maggie had a point. But how was Kaitlyn going to explain the rumor to her mother?

"Next problem," Maggie said. "Advertising."

"How about a billboard?" said Liesel.

"Sounds expensive," said Kaitlyn. "And kind of . . . big."

Liesel shrugged. "I was thinking it would be fun to paint."

"What about a leaflet?" said Maggie. "You could put them on people's doorsteps and stuff."

"Like a takeout menu?" Liesel said. "She's a baby-sitter, not a Chinese restaurant."

"No, but that's not a bad idea," Kaitlyn said. "A menu of babysitting services."

"And it could list different add-ons. You know, like side dishes. You could bake cookies, or throw little parties. . . ." Maggie suggested.

"It could have a really cool design," Liesel added, warming to the idea.

"Or cook dinner." Maggie was practically bouncing up and down in her seat.

Kaitlyn frowned. "I can't cook. Unless you count popping cinnamon rolls out of a can and sticking them in the oven."

"What else can you do?" asked Maggie.

Kaitlyn thought for a moment. "I'm pretty good at cleaning," she said. "I mean, half the time when I babysit, I end up cleaning, anyway."

"Good. We'll add that to the menu," Maggie said. She had already started jotting down notes on a piece of paper. "Liesel, can you make this into a cool design?"

"No problem," said Liesel.

"Okay, Liesel and I will start working on the flyer. Kaitlyn, you go talk to your mom about the rumor," Maggie instructed in her take-charge voice.

"Now?"

Maggie looked at her. "When else?"

Kaitlyn reluctantly got up from the table. "Don't eat all the cinnamon rolls without me," she said.

Maggie and Liesel nodded, barely looking up from the flyer.

With a sigh, Kaitlyn went to go find her mother.

"Mom?" Kaitlyn ducked her head into the living room. She hoped she would find her mother on the phone.

No such luck. Mrs. Sweeney was reading a magazine.

"Mmm?" her mother murmured.

"Can I talk to you?"

"Sure, honey. What's up?" Mrs. Sweeney asked without lifting her eyes from the page.

Kaitlyn settled into a reading chair next to her. "Um, well, this weird thing happened. . . ."

Mrs. Sweeney put down the magazine and looked at Kaitlyn. "That doesn't sound good."

"I didn't do anything," Kaitlyn said quickly. "It's just . . . well, I haven't gotten very many calls to babysit lately. So I called a couple people — you know, the Browns and the Davises — just to say hi. And it turns out there's this weird rumor going around that I have mono."

"Mono!" said Mrs. Sweeney.

Kaitlyn nodded.

"Why on earth do they think you have mono?"

"I have no idea!" Kaitlyn said, her eyes widening. It wasn't exactly a lie.

Mrs. Sweeney studied her daughter. "Who have you been kissing?"

"What?!" Kaitlyn looked at her mother in horror. What was she talking about?

"They call mono 'the kissing disease,'" her mother explained. The corners of her mouth twitched. "Supposedly you get it from kissing."

"I haven't been kissing *anyone*!" Kaitlyn said truthfully. She'd never even come *close* to kissing someone. At the moment, though, she didn't know which was more embarrassing — never having kissed a boy, or actually discussing it with her mother.

"All right," Kaitlyn's mother said. Kaitlyn could tell she was trying not to laugh, which somehow made it worse. "So what about this mono you have?"

"Well, I think that's the reason I haven't been getting any babysitting jobs," Kaitlyn said, eager to move off the subject of kissing. "So I was hoping maybe you could let some of the parents know that I don't have mono. You know, just mention in a conversation that I'm perfectly healthy and not contagious in any way."

Her mother smiled. "I could probably do that."

"Thanks, Mom." Kaitlyn got up from the chair and headed for the door before her mother could bring up any more embarrassing topics.

Back in the kitchen, she found Maggie and Liesel had almost finished a hand-drawn flyer.

"See what you think," Maggie said.

Kaitlyn looked over her shoulder. The flyer read:

You've tried the rest
Now go with the best
Kaitlyn Sweeney
The housecleaning babysitter!
* Great prices * Great references *
Plus, get your whole house cleaned!
MENU OF SERVICES
Giggles, games, and great babysitting . . . included in cost
Dishwashing......add $1
Vacuuming......add $2
Laundry......add $3

**With 4 or more hours of babysitting,
get your house cleaned for free!**

On the bottom of the page, Liesel had drawn a girl who looked like Kaitlyn. She was holding hands with two kids, who were holding hands with more kids. They made a border all the way around the edge of the page.

Kaitlyn pointed to the last line. "What's this?"

Maggie smiled. "That's the hook! Good idea, right? I figured they shouldn't get their house cleaned if they only hired you for one hour."

Kaitlyn nodded slowly. "Do you think we could change it to say, 'Get your whole house cleaned for just five dollars'?"

"I guess that's still a good deal." Maggie erased "free" and wrote in "five dollars." Then she stood up. "Ready to get your babysitting business back?"

Kaitlyn grinned. "You bet I am."

Chapter Nine

By Saturday night, Kaitlyn had gotten three calls from people who'd seen her flyer. It had been out less than twenty-four hours, and she was already getting new customers. At this rate, business was going to be better than ever!

"Take that, Nola!" Kaitlyn said to herself as she wrote down the address of a family who wanted her to sit the next afternoon.

On Sunday, she rode her bike to the address the mother had given her over the phone. It was a small, cozy-looking white house in an older part of town. Kaitlyn parked her bike at the side of the house, then went around to the front and rang the doorbell.

A frizzy-haired woman answered the door. She was carrying a baby wearing a food-stained bib.

"Are you the housecleaning babysitter?" she asked.

"That's me," Kaitlyn said with a smile.

"You'll clean the whole house for just five dollars?" The woman looked like she didn't believe it.

"That's right."

The woman swung the door open wide. "Come on in."

The moment she stepped inside the house, Kaitlyn realized she had made a mistake. To begin with, the house looked much smaller on the outside than it was on the inside. The living room was at least twice the size of Kaitlyn's. And it was a disaster zone! Toy cars, dolls, balls, stuffed animals, baby rattles, and countless other playthings were scattered like corpses on a battlefield. It looked like someone had picked up a whole toy store and shaken the contents out on the living room floor.

The woman didn't seem to notice anything wrong. She stepped lightly over a stuffed alligator and headed for the back of the house. Kaitlyn followed with a sinking heart.

"This is Max," the mother said, plunking the baby into his high chair. The tray in front of him was smeared with green mush that matched the mess on his bib. "He's having peas for lunch."

"Hi, Max," Kaitlyn said weakly.

"And this is Julia and Charles," the mother said, nodding to two small children who were sitting at the kitchen table, eating peanut-butter-and-jelly sandwiches. "Guys, this is Kaitlyn. She's our new babysitter. Say hello."

"Hello," Julia and Charles chorused.

Kaitlyn barely noticed. She was too busy taking in the sticky plates and half-eaten bowls of cereal that covered the table, the dirty glasses in the sink, and the toys and newspapers scattered on the floor.

Charles reached for his glass of milk and knocked it over.

"Oops," he said. A puddle of milk spread across the table and dripped onto the floor.

"Oh, honey," said his mother. "Kaitlyn, could you take care of that? I've got to go. I'm going to be late for my appointment."

She grabbed her purse off the counter and hustled out of the room, calling back over her shoulder, "The emergency numbers are on the fridge. I should be back around five. Bye-bye!"

For a moment, Kaitlyn just stood there watching the milk drip onto the floor. She thought, *I am going to kill Maggie for this!*

"I want more milk," Charles whined.

Kaitlyn shook herself out of her daze. She found

the milk carton, which was sitting open on the counter, and refilled Charles's glass. Then she put the carton in the fridge and turned to Julia. "Where does your mom keep the mop?"

Julia stared at her.

"The mop?" Kaitlyn pantomimed mopping. Julia pointed to a cupboard.

Inside, Kaitlyn found a mop and bucket buried behind a mountain of plastic grocery bags. While she filled the bucket with water, she loaded some of the dirty dishes into the dishwasher. She couldn't believe how many dishes there were. It was like they'd had the U.S. Army over for breakfast.

Julia got down from her chair and came to supervise. "My mom doesn't put the bowls there," she said.

"Oh yeah? Where does she put them?" Kaitlyn snapped. "Oh, wait, let me guess. She puts them in the *sink*, so when the babysitter comes, *she* can take care of them." She slammed another bowl into the dishwasher.

Julia's eyes widened.

Kaitlyn sighed. *It's not this poor kid's fault I'm stuck cleaning up this pigsty,* she thought. "Where does she put them?" she asked in a nicer tone.

The girl pointed to the rack Kaitlyn had just filled with glasses.

Whatever. Kaitlyn wasn't going to reload the dishwasher just so the bowls could be in the right place. She shut the dishwasher and turned it on.

Kaitlyn took the full bucket of water from the sink and began to mop up the spilled milk. When she moved to mop under Charles's chair, he kicked the handle.

"Stop it, Charles," she said.

Charles giggled. He kicked the mop again.

"I mean it, Charles," Kaitlyn said. She held Charles's feet in one hand and finished mopping with the other.

Charles laughed. Max squealed and flung some mashed peas onto the floor where Kaitlyn had just finished mopping.

The rest of the day was the same. As fast as Kaitlyn cleaned the house, the kids messed it up again. It was like trying to shovel a sidewalk during a blizzard, Kaitlyn thought. Completely pointless.

Finally, she managed to get most of the toys into a shaky pile in the corner of the living room. She made the beds. She shoved the kids' scattered shoes and clothes into their bedroom closets.

Kaitlyn was just wiping off Max's high chair tray when their mother walked in the door. Kaitlyn almost didn't recognize her. She was wearing fresh lipstick, and her hands were full of department store bags. She looked like she'd had her hair done.

"Mommy!" Julia cried, jumping up from the floor in front of the television. Charles stayed where he was, his eyes glued to *The Little Mermaid* DVD that was playing.

Kaitlyn glanced guiltily at their mother. She considered it poor form to park the kids in front of a DVD while she was babysitting. But it was the only way she could get them to sit still long enough for her to clean the house.

The mother didn't seem to mind. Kaitlyn guessed she probably used the DVD trick all the time.

"Hi, sweetie," the mother said to Julia. She took Max into her arms. "Everything go okay?"

Kaitlyn just nodded. She was too tired to even bother with the full report.

"She put the bowls in the wrong place," Julia informed her mother.

Kaitlyn glowered at her.

The mother glanced around the living room. Kaitlyn proudly followed her gaze. She'd practically worked a miracle in there. She almost expected the woman to get down on her knees and weep with gratitude.

Instead, the mother reached for her purse. "So, I owe you for four hours."

"Yes," said Kaitlyn. "Plus the five dollars for cleaning."

The woman pulled a few bills out of her purse. "Just a second," she said. "I'm going to have to get some money from the other room."

She went down the hall, still carrying Max. A moment later she returned.

"You didn't clean the bathroom," she said.

"What?" Kaitlyn asked, startled.

"The bathroom. There are towels on the floor and it doesn't look like the toilet has been properly scrubbed."

Kaitlyn just stared at her, speechless.

"I'll pay for the babysitting. But I'm only going to give you three dollars for cleaning," the woman said, carefully counting out the bills, "since you didn't do the whole house."

Kaitlyn pressed her lips together and silently took the money. It was all she could do to keep from snatching it out of the woman's hand.

Outside, her eyes filled with angry tears. Three dollars! She'd busted her behind in there for three measly bucks! And that woman had the nerve to act like Kaitlyn was trying to cheat her.

And she would probably never call Kaitlyn

again. Well, she didn't care. She didn't want to baby-sit for people like that!

Kaitlyn arrived back at her house exhausted. All she wanted to do was take a shower, put on her oldest, coziest pajamas, and park *herself* in front of the TV.

"Kaitlyn!" Lily appeared in the doorway of Kaitlyn's room.

"Go away, Lily," she said. She wasn't in the mood to entertain.

"Somebody called," Lily reported.

"Who?" Kaitlyn asked. Her friends and most of her babysitting clients knew to call her on her cell phone.

"A bo-o-oy," Lily trilled.

Kaitlyn's heart skipped a beat. "What boy?"

"He said he'd call back."

Kaitlyn raced to the phone to check the caller ID. "WALKER," it read. And there — she could hardly believe her eyes — was Topher's number!

"He called!" Kaitlyn shouted. She was no longer tired. She felt like she could run a hundred miles.

Lily had followed her into the room and was watching her with amazement. Kaitlyn grabbed her sister's hands and danced her around. "He called!" she sang.

Suddenly the terrible babysitting job didn't

matter so much. She didn't care how rude the mother had been. Or that she'd worked her fingers to the bone for three dollars. For a second, just a second, she even forgot about Nola.

Topher Walker had called her, and that could only mean one thing: Topher liked her! And now Kaitlyn couldn't deny that she liked him, too.

Chapter Ten

Kaitlyn waited all Sunday night for Topher to call her back, but the call never came. Monday in Spanish class, she stared at the back of his head, willing him to turn around. In between issuing telepathic commands, she tried to think of how she might bring up the phone call.

So, Topher, do anything special last night?

No.

Topher, it was the weirdest thing, but somebody called our house last night with the exact same last name as you. Isn't that funny?

No.

Topher Walker, can you tell me what you were doing at exactly 6:22 P.M. on the evening of March twenty-sixth?

But Topher seemed to have a skull made of

steel. As far as Kaitlyn could tell, not a single one of her thought waves was getting through to his brain. The only person who *was* picking them up was Señora Ramos. She called on Kaitlyn twice.

After an agonizingly long fifty minutes, Kaitlyn decided to take matters into her own hands. When the bell rang, she scooped up her books and followed Topher to the door.

"Hey, Topher."

"Hey!" He seemed surprised. For a second Kaitlyn wondered if he hadn't called her after all. But she'd seen his number!

Now what? Kaitlyn's mind went blank. She said the first thing that came to mind: "Your shoe's untied."

Topher looked down. "Oh. Thanks." He tied his shoe.

"Well," he said, standing up. "Later."

Note to self, Kaitlyn thought as she watched him walk away, *next time let him trip and fall.* At least then maybe she'd have a way to start a conversation — or at least a captive audience.

Twice in the days that followed, Señora Ramos did dialogue exercises, and both times Topher was Kaitlyn's partner. Each time, they tried to top each other's stories. She told him about the Monster in a story that exhausted both her Spanish vocabulary and her improvisational miming skills. He told her a story that involved a free-throw shot and a buzzing bee. Or was it his ears that were buzzing? She couldn't tell if he meant to say *abeja* or *orejas.* Either way, it was funny. They both ended up laughing so hard they were crying.

But whenever she saw him in the hallways, all Topher said was "Hey." He never mentioned the phone call. And he never called back.

"He likes you," Maggie said. Maggie was an eternal optimist.

Kaitlyn wasn't sure. Did he like her? Did he like Nola? She had seen them one other time, talking by the water fountain. They had been talking just as intensely as the first time Kaitlyn had seen them.

Kaitlyn didn't know what to believe. One thing was for sure, Topher was turning out to be a real mystery.

By the weekend, it was clear that Topher wasn't going to call again. Maybe he hadn't meant to call the first time, Kaitlyn thought. Maybe he had accidentally misdialed.

Or maybe he was just calling to get the Spanish homework.

Or maybe . . . maybe he was prank calling her. As a joke! Kaitlyn hoped that wasn't true. The thought was too horrible.

She considered all these possibilities Sunday afternoon, while she sat for the Monster again. After last weekend's exhausting, miserable job, Kaitlyn had given up the housecleaning idea. But she wasn't giving up on babysitting — not even close. She was still determined to make the Wonder World trip happen. Besides, she couldn't just walk away and let Nola win! From then on, she was going to take every job she could get — even if it meant babysitting the Monster.

Kaitlyn sat on the Arnolds' kitchen floor, watching the Monster smear finger paint on a large piece of newsprint.

This isn't so bad. He's actually a pretty cute kid when he's not screaming, she thought.

"Watch, Troy," she said. "This is how you make a handprint." She took his hand and dipped it in the paint, then pressed it against the paper.

The Monster seemed impressed. He dipped his other hand in the paint and smacked the paper.

"Good job," said Kaitlyn.

The Monster grinned. He dipped both hands in the paint, then turned and smacked Kaitlyn's shirt.

"No, Troy!" Kaitlyn said. She pulled her T-shirt

away from her to inspect the damage. His hands had left two blue smears right across the logo on the front. Quickly she checked the paint jar and saw with relief that the paint was washable.

"You have to paint on the paper," she told the toddler. She pressed his hand against the newsprint again. Troy swung his other gooey hand around and smacked the side of her head.

"Ow! Troy! That's enough!"

But the Monster was just getting started. He stood up and stepped onto his painting. Then he began to stomp all around it, leaving a trail of multicolored footprints.

So much for cute, Kaitlyn thought. *I should have known that would last about one second.*

"Okay. I think that's enough painting for one day." Kaitlyn scooped up the paints and paper and carried them over to the sink.

"Mine!" the Monster shrieked.

"Nope, we're done, kiddo," Kaitlyn said firmly.

Troy's lower lip trembled.

"No tantrums," Kaitlyn warned him.

Troy opened his mouth and screamed.

Kaitlyn covered her ears. *The Arnolds could make some extra money leasing this kid to the fire department,* she thought. His scream was definitely louder than any siren she'd ever heard.

Fifteen minutes later, Troy was still shrieking like a smoke alarm, and Kaitlyn felt like screaming herself.

"Come on, Troy. We're going to the park," she said. At least there the noise would be diffused in the open air. She hoped so, anyway.

Apparently Troy liked the idea of the park, too. His wailing downgraded to regular crying. By the time Kaitlyn found his shoes and coat, he had quieted to a whimper.

The moment she opened the door, Troy slipped past her and took off running.

"No, Troy! Stop!"

Kaitlyn caught him just before he reached the curb. Her heart was pounding. The kid had nearly run into the street!

"Hold my hand," she instructed.

But Troy didn't want to hold her hand. Every time she got hold of him, he slithered out of her grip.

So Kaitlyn was forced to carry him the three blocks to the park. The Monster screamed like a torture victim the whole way. Kaitlyn tried to ignore the looks she got from the people she passed on the sidewalk. She was grateful that none of the other families she sat for lived on this street.

It was the first real spring day, and the park was

full of parents and kids. Several heads turned as Kaitlyn and Troy arrived.

Cheeks burning, she set the Monster down on the grass. "Okay, kiddo. We're at the park. You can run wherever you want."

The Monster continued to cry.

"Come on, Troy, let's go to the sandbox. Or the swings? How about the swings?" Kaitlyn could hear herself starting to sound desperate.

The only response was a howl.

"All right. That's enough, Troy," Kaitlyn said sharply. "If you don't stop crying, we're going back home."

Wrong thing to say. Troy's wailing increased by several decibels. A few parents looked over and frowned. The thought flashed through Kaitlyn's mind that if he didn't stop soon, someone might report her for noise pollution.

She tried to pick the Monster up. He went limp, slid through her hands, and collapsed in a heap at her feet.

Kaitlyn was considering whether she could drag him home by the hood of his coat, when she heard someone behind her say, "Kaitlyn?"

Kaitlyn turned. *This can't be happening,* she thought. "Nola," she said. "What a surprise."

Nola smiled. She was wearing a pink top and crisp khaki pants. As usual, she looked like she'd walked straight off the pages of a Ralph Lauren catalog. A pair of equally catalog-worthy little girls in matching pink coats stood at her sides, their hands tucked firmly into hers. Kaitlyn was suddenly keenly aware of her paint-smeared hair and clothes. Never mind the howling banshee at her feet.

"I thought that was you," said Nola. "Isn't it a beautiful day? I just couldn't wait to come over to the park." She had to speak loudly to be heard above the Monster's wailing.

Kaitlyn nodded. The competing emotions of anger and embarrassment were keeping her from forming a proper sentence.

"Do you know the twins?" Nola asked.

Kaitlyn finally found her voice. "Yes, I've baby-sat for them before." She looked down at the little girls. "Hi, Tiffy. Hi, Tasha."

The twins didn't even acknowledge her. They were staring at the Monster in silent fascination.

"And who's this little guy?" Nola asked in a babyish voice.

"That," said Kaitlyn, "is Troy. Careful," she added as Nola knelt down next to him. "He might explode."

Nola laughed like that was the funniest thing

she'd heard all day. "Hi, Troy," she said in a sing-songy voice. "Are you feeling grumpy today?"

The Monster wailed in reply.

Good boy, Troy, thought Kaitlyn. She wanted him to stop crying, but she didn't want him to do it on account of Nola.

"That's too bad," Nola said, still in her nursery-rhyme voice. "I guess that means you won't be able to play in my bluegrass band." She reached over and plucked a blade of grass from the lawn. Then she put it between her thumbs and blew on it. The grass made a noise like a kazoo.

The Monster paused.

Nola pretended not to notice. She blew on the grass a few more times.

The Monster sat up. He reached over and tugged at her hands, wanting to see what was making the noise.

Nola acted surprised. "Oh! You *do* want to be in my bluegrass band!" She showed him the blade of grass.

"Do it again, Nola!" one of the twins cried. Nola blew on the grass again. The Monster laughed and clapped his hands. Kaitlyn glared at him. The little traitor.

"You didn't need to do that," she told Nola. "I was totally handling it."

Nola glanced up at her. "I just thought you could use some help. Sometimes the best thing to do when a kid has a temper tantrum is distract him."

I know what you thought, you egotistical show-off, Kaitlyn silently growled.

"Nola, come play on the swings!" one of the twins cried, tugging at her hand.

"Come on, come on!" her sister echoed.

Nola smiled at her adoring fans. "Kaitlyn, do you guys want to come?"

I would rather eat worms, thought Kaitlyn. "We have to go home soon," she said.

"Well, good luck," Nola replied in a way that set Kaitlyn's teeth on edge. She took off toward the swing set, with the twins skipping along beside her.

Outrageous! Kaitlyn fumed. She couldn't believe Nola had tried to show her up right to her own face!

No way was Kaitlyn going to just sit back and let Nola take her place as the town's favorite baby-sitter. This wasn't just business. Now it was war.

Chapter Eleven

As far as Kaitlyn was concerned, nothing was out of the question in the battle for babysitting business. She was prepared for vicious rumors, evil stares, underground acts of sabotage.

So she was astonished when Nola walked right up to her in the hallway at school on Monday morning.

"Hi, Kaitlyn," Nola said pleasantly.

"Hello, Nola," Kaitlyn replied in an icy voice.

Nola didn't seem to notice. "So, how'd it go yesterday?"

So that was it. Nola had come to rub the trouble with the Monster in Kaitlyn's face.

She's trying to get to you, said a little voice in Kaitlyn's brain. *She wants to see you squirm. Don't show any sign of weakness.*

She gave Nola a confident smile. "Great!"

"Cool," said Nola. "I meant to tell you, I babysat for these people named the Johnsons last week. They said they knew you."

Behind her smile, Kaitlyn's teeth clenched.

"Aren't little Joey and Katie the cutest kids ever?" said Nola.

"They're cute," Kaitlyn agreed. *She's trying to get your secrets. Don't give anything away!* she warned herself. She turned and began to rummage in her locker, signaling that the conversation was over.

Nola lingered for a moment. "Well, I just saw you standing over here, so I thought I'd come over and say hey," she said at last.

"Mm-hmm," Kaitlyn said without looking up.

Kaitlyn dug around in her locker some more, but Nola still didn't move. What was this girl's problem? Kaitlyn wondered. At last, she turned and raised her eyebrows at Nola to say, *Why are you still here?*

For the first time, a look of uncertainty flashed across Nola's face. "Um, I guess I'll see you around, then."

"See ya." Kaitlyn shook her head as she watched Nola walk away. She couldn't believe how two-faced Nola had acted. The girl had some nerve!

"What was that about?" Maggie asked, walking over.

"She's trying to sabotage me," Kaitlyn said. She gave Maggie a brief rundown of what had happened in the park. "She just came out of nowhere and took over, like she owned the place."

"Wow," Maggie said. "It's weird, she seems so sweet."

"It's just an act," Kaitlyn assured her. "She was totally trying to show me up in front of all the parents yesterday. Like if she steals all my clients behind my back I'll just roll over and admit defeat?"

"She obviously doesn't know who she's dealing with," Maggie said.

"Obviously not," Kaitlyn agreed. She slammed her locker so hard Maggie flinched.

"By the way, I was thinking we should do something for Liesel," Kaitlyn said, as they started down the hall. "Since her art show is on Friday."

"That's a good idea," Maggie said. "Maybe we can go shopping for something after school tomorrow. Nothing too expensive," she added quickly.

"Right," Kaitlyn agreed. "Just something to let her know how much we think she rocks."

* * *

All that morning, Kaitlyn stewed about her run-in with Nola. As she sat through her classes, she fantasized about ways to get back at her.

In science, she thought about pouring Coke through the vents in Nola's locker.

In social studies, she considered sending a love note to the nerdiest boy in the seventh grade and signing Nola's name.

In English, she imagined sending a love note to the most *popular* boy in the class and signing Nola's name.

But every idea she had seemed silly and immature. The truth was she didn't just want to get back at Nola. She wanted to win the babysitting war. And she wanted Nola to surrender.

After school that day, Kaitlyn was in the library, looking for a book for her English class, when she rounded a corner and saw Nola. She was sitting at a table with her back to Kaitlyn, her long hair falling to one side as she leaned over a notebook.

Just as Kaitlyn was about to turn and go the other way, Nola stood up. At first Kaitlyn thought she was just stretching. But Nola walked past the front desk and out to the hallway, leaving her books on the table. Probably headed for the bathroom, Kaitlyn thought.

Kaitlyn sidled over to the table where Nola had been sitting. A math book was open to a set of algebra problems. Kaitlyn studied Nola's notebook and saw with satisfaction that she'd made a mistake on the very first one.

Blip! An electronic beep almost made Kaitlyn jump out of her skin. She looked down and saw Nola's cell phone on the floor, where it had fallen from her coat. A light on the phone blinked.

Kaitlyn glanced over at the door. There was no sign of Nola.

Casually, she bent down, as if she were tying her shoelace. She picked up Nola's phone and flipped it open.

There was a text message from Mrs. Brown. Hardly believing what she was doing, Kaitlyn opened it. It read, CAN U COME AT 6 INSTD OF 7 2NITE? -MRS. B.

Kaitlyn sucked in her breath. Here was her chance to get back at Nola, practically handed to her on a silver platter. It was almost too easy.

Too easy, Kaitlyn thought, but was it also too mean? She paused, her thumb hovering above the keypad.

Nola's smug expression in the park the day before flashed through her mind. *All's fair in love and war,* Kaitlyn reminded herself. *Especially war.*

OK, she typed.

Before she could think more about it, she hit SEND and placed the phone back under Nola's chair.

Immediately, she felt guilty. Kaitlyn knew she was competitive, but she always played fair. And what she had just done was definitely not fair. But what could she do about it now?

As she stood there considering, she heard someone say her name.

Kaitlyn's head jerked up. Topher was walking toward her.

"What's up?" he asked.

"Nothing!" Kaitlyn blurted. She hoped he hadn't noticed her messing with Nola's phone. She added, a little more casually, "I was just getting a book for English. What's up with you?"

"Not much," said Topher. "I'm meeting some-one here."

Kaitlyn's gaze fell to the notebook on the table. *Could that someone be Nola?* she wondered. Her stomach dropped.

Suddenly, Kaitlyn was dying to get out of there. She didn't want to have to see Nola and Topher together when Nola got back. And she didn't want Nola to catch her anywhere near her phone.

"I gotta go," she said to Topher, and bolted toward the library door.

In the hallway Kaitlyn saw Nola on her way back from the bathroom. They locked eyes as they passed each other.

Kaitlyn felt torn between guilt and satisfaction. She shouldn't have done it.

But on the other hand, she thought, *Nola definitely had it coming.*

Chapter Twelve

Kaitlyn lay on Liesel's bed, painting her fingernails with blue polish that she'd found on Liesel's desk. Liesel and Maggie were standing in front of the full-length mirror. It was the night before Liesel's art show, and Kaitlyn and Maggie had come over to make sure she was ready.

"Maybe you should try it up," said Maggie. She swept Liesel's hair up onto the back of her head.

Liesel frowned. "It makes my neck look too long."

Maggie let her hair fall back down. "What about a French braid?"

"You guys will never believe what happened on the way over here," Kaitlyn said from the bed. "I was at the grocery store with my mom and we ran into some people she knows. Their kid was wearing this T-shirt that said, 'I love my babysitter, Nola,' with a big picture of Nola's face! Can you believe it? She hands T-shirts out to the kids she sits for so they can advertise for her. Isn't that the stupidest thing you've ever heard?"

Maggie and Liesel glanced at each other.

Kaitlyn caught their look. "What?"

"It's just . . ." Maggie began.

"We're sick of hearing about Nola," Liesel said firmly.

"What?" Kaitlyn looked from Liesel to Maggie.

"She's *all* you talk about anymore," Liesel went on. "It's like you've become totally obsessed with beating her at babysitting — which, last I checked, isn't a competition."

"I can't help it. She's stealing my clients!" Kaitlyn exclaimed. "Why are you taking her side all of a sudden?"

"We're not taking her side. We just don't understand why you care so much," Maggie said, not unkindly. "I mean, do you even *like* babysitting?"

"Of course I do!"

"Why?"

"Why what? Why do I like babysitting?"

Maggie nodded.

Kaitlyn paused. Why *did* she like babysitting? She certainly didn't like changing diapers, or dealing with temper tantrums, or mopping the kitchen floor after some kid had spilled his milk.

She liked the money she got from babysitting, and she liked hearing that she was good at it. But she knew those weren't the reasons Maggie was looking for. Liking money and praise wasn't the same as liking babysitting.

Maggie and Liesel were looking at her, waiting for an answer.

"I just do," Kaitlyn said lamely.

Liesel sighed. "Well, if you want to be the best babysitter around, you should start *acting* like the best."

"What do you mean?" asked Kaitlyn.

"I mean, you keep freaking out every time you think Nola might be getting more jobs than you. But a really good babysitter wouldn't care. She would just know she was the best, and then people would treat her like she was the best. It's like with art," Liesel continued. "If you start worrying about what everybody else is painting, and thinking, 'That cow they painted is better than my cow,' then you'll never be able to paint anything. But if you just paint what you want and it comes from inside you, then your cow really *will* be the most amazing, unique cow painting in the world, and people will love it and want to pay hundreds of dollars for it."

"Are you saying I should charge hundreds of dollars?" Kaitlyn asked.

"I'm *saying* you should start acting like you're worth it," Liesel replied.

"Okay, enough already," Maggie piped up. "No offense, Kaitlyn, but can we stop talking about babysitting for a minute? Tomorrow is Liesel's big night."

Liesel grinned. "Wait till you see the dress."

"What did you do to it?" Maggie asked, aghast. "You didn't get paint on it, did you?"

"You'll see." Liesel slipped out of the room. She came back a moment later, wearing the black velvet dress.

Maggie and Kaitlyn both gasped.

"It fits you perfectly!" cried Kaitlyn.

"My mom had it taken in for me," Liesel told them. She did a little spin for her friends.

"I brought shoes," said Maggie. She pulled a pair of black heels from a shopping bag. "They're practically new. I only wore them once, to my cousin's wedding."

Liesel slipped them on. "What do you think?"

"Very mature," said Kaitlyn. "But it needs something."

She went over to her backpack and got out a little box. "It's from Maggie and me," she said, handing it to Liesel.

Inside was a silver necklace with a tiny horseshoe charm. "For luck," Kaitlyn explained.

"You guys are the best," Liesel said, giving each of her friends a hug. She went to the mirror to put the necklace on. "It's perfect. And now I have something for you guys."

"What is it?" asked Maggie, surprised.

"You, my friends, are going to be the first people on the planet to get a look at the latest masterpiece by Liesel Von Graff."

"Really?" Kaitlyn and Maggie said in unison. Liesel nodded.

She led them to the kitchen. The painting was leaning up against a wall, covered by a cloth.

"Drumroll, please," said Liesel. Maggie improvised a drumroll on the table.

"Da-da-da-DAH!" Liesel whipped away the cloth. Kaitlyn and Maggie stared.

"It's us," Maggie said after a moment. The painting was done in bright, crazy colors. Kaitlyn's skin was hot pink and her hair was purple. Maggie was blue with bright yellow hair. And Liesel had painted herself in orange and green. But it was undeniably them.

"It's so good, Liesel," Kaitlyn said.

Liesel put her arms around her friends' shoulders, just like they were in the picture. "I had lots of inspiration," she said.

Chapter Thirteen

Kaitlyn decided to follow Liesel's advice. On her own, she made up a new flyer, using the most elegant font she could find on her computer. It said simply:

Kaitlyn Sweeney

Quality Care for infants, toddlers, and children

Excellent references

Then it listed her cell phone and home phone numbers. Kaitlyn decided not to put a price on the flyer. She thought it seemed more sophisticated that way.

Next, Kaitlyn found her mom's PTA list, which

had the names and addresses of all the families whose kids attended the elementary school. She mailed the flyers to only a few families. No more scattering leaflets on random doorsteps. She was going to start being selective about who she sat for!

Now there was just one more thing to do: It was time to meet the enemy head-on.

Friday afternoon, she saw Nola standing at her locker. Kaitlyn marched over to her. "Nola," she said, with as much civility as she could muster.

Nola turned around. "Hi, Kaitlyn," she said. She seemed surprised.

"So." Kaitlyn folded her arms across her chest. "I guess you've been doing a lot of babysitting lately."

"Um, yeah. I guess I have been doing kind of a lot." Nola looked at Kaitlyn like she wasn't sure where this was going.

"You babysit for the Browns and the Knopfskys and the Nichols and the Parkers and the Davises, right?"

Nola nodded. She opened her mouth to say something, but Kaitlyn plowed ahead. She was going to prove once and for all that she knew the kids better than anyone, except possibly their own parents.

"So I guess you know that Mindy Brown's favorite book is *One Fish, Two Fish, Red Fish, Blue Fish,* right? And that Nick Davis wets the bed unless you leave the night-light on. And that Jolie Parker has to have her sandwiches cut into triangles or she won't eat them."

Nola blinked. Kaitlyn decided to press her advantage.

"And I guess you'd never even dream of giving Nathan Knopfsky permission to have his friend Billy over, because you know they'll make a colossal mess." Kaitlyn's eyes burrowed into Nola's. "And you're perfectly aware that little Belle Nichols has to be burped *three times* before you put her down, or *she'll* make a mess."

To Kaitlyn's surprise, Nola suddenly laughed.

"And how about Melissa Davis?" she said, grinning at Kaitlyn. "Isn't it funny how she'll only wear pink socks, and if you try to get her to wear any other color, she throws a fit?"

Kaitlyn stared at her. What was going on? Nola was supposed to be intimidated — she wasn't supposed to play along! Was Nola actually trying to one-up her?

"And Rosie Bailey," Nola went on, "isn't she a little cutie, the way she has all her books memorized and recites them with you as you read?"

Now it was Kaitlyn's turn to be startled. "You babysit for Rosie Bailey?"

"Yeah," said Nola, "in fact, I'm sitting for her again this afternoon."

Kaitlyn took a step back. She couldn't believe it. Just weeks before, the Baileys had practically been begging Kaitlyn to come babysit for them.

And now they had jumped on the Nola bandwagon, too.

"What's wrong, Kaitlyn?" asked Nola. But Kaitlyn barely heard her. She walked away, feeling stunned.

Why was it that everyone wanted Nola to sit for them? What was so special about her? Kaitlyn had to know.

And suddenly she thought of a way she could find out.

Chapter Fourteen

As the station wagon pulled up in front of the Baileys' house, Kaitlyn kept an anxious watch out the passenger-side window. She didn't want anyone inside the house to see her get out of the car.

"Are you going to need a ride home, or will the Baileys bring you?" Mrs. Sweeney asked from the driver's seat.

Kaitlyn checked her watch. It was 4:30. Liesel's art show started at six. Kaitlyn's mother would never believe she was only sitting for an hour. It would be better to call Maggie when she was done here, and ask her to pick her up on her way downtown to the museum. Then she could catch a lift home with Maggie's or Liesel's parents.

"I'll get a ride," she told her mother.

Kaitlyn opened the door and got out. She waved

good-bye and started up the walkway, as if she were going to the front door. She kept her fingers crossed that no one was looking out the windows.

As soon as the car pulled away, Kaitlyn veered right and headed for the side of the house. Her plan was to hide in the flower bushes by the kitchen window. There she would be able to see inside, but she would still be hidden from the street.

"Ow!" Kaitlyn whispered as the thorns on a cluster of rosebushes snagged her skin. She hunkered down in the bushes, regretting that she hadn't worn a thicker sweater. She hadn't remembered the plants here being quite so prickly!

Kaitlyn felt something jab into her hip and realized it was her cell phone. She pulled it out and turned it off. The last thing she needed was to get a call when she was hiding in the bushes like some cat burglar.

As soon as she found a somewhat comfortable position, she peeped over the edge of the window ledge.

Oh! There was Nola!

She was talking to Mrs. Bailey. Kaitlyn couldn't hear what they were saying, but she could tell by the earnest look on Nola's face that she was probably getting instructions.

Kaitlyn knew that look. She often used it herself.

Mrs. Bailey kissed little Rosie and left through the front door. Rosie started to cry. Kaitlyn could hear her even through the closed window.

Ha! she thought. *Let's see how Nola handles this one.*

Nola knelt down and said something to Rosie. Then she reached under the table and pulled up an enormous rainbow-colored duffel bag.

Who does she think she is? thought Kaitlyn. *Mary Poppins?*

Still half crying, Rosie watched curiously as Nola fished around inside the bag.

With a flourish, the babysitter produced a pair of costume fairy wings and a little crown made of silk flowers. She placed the crown on Rosie's head and helped her slip her arms through the wings. Rosie was definitely not crying now. The little girl looked like she might actually combust from sheer delight.

Okay, Kaitlyn grudgingly admitted. *So she has a good bag of tricks.*

Brwowowowowowowowowow!

A volley of barking suddenly burst from inside the Baileys' house. Brutus, the family dachshund, trotted over to the window and looked out at Kaitlyn.

She shrank down in the bushes. "Shhh. Brutus, it's just me. Go away," she pleaded.

"Brwowowowowowowowow!" said Brutus.

Nola glanced toward the window. A second later, she had scooped the dog up and carried him to the back door. "Out you go," Kaitlyn heard Nola say. The door closed behind him.

Brutus ran around and joined Kaitlyn in the bushes. "Good dog," she said, patting his head. "Good dog. Now be quiet."

Brutus cooperated. Kaitlyn watched through the window as Nola put on a CD and danced around the kitchen with Rosie. They applied temporary tattoos. They made bakeless cookies out of healthy ingredients like peanut butter and cornflakes, which — Kaitlyn was sorry to note — Rosie seemed to find delicious. Nola even somehow made a game out of loading the dishwasher.

By the time Nola pulled finger puppets out of her bag and started to put on a show, Rosie was looking at her like she was some kind of goddess. Kaitlyn had to admit Nola certainly had some clever babysitting tricks — and Kaitlyn planned to use them the first chance she got.

Kaitlyn's hands were cold and her legs were starting to cramp. She was just considering going back out to the street and calling Maggie for a ride, when Brutus, who'd been curled up by her side, suddenly jumped to his feet and began to bark.

"Shhhhhhhh!" Kaitlyn put a hand on the dog to quiet him, but it was no use. Brutus kept barking.

A second later, the doorbell rang.

Nola went to answer the door. When she returned, she had someone with her. Kaitlyn craned her neck, but a cabinet blocked her view of the visitor. All she could see was the sleeve of a jacket.

Kaitlyn's eyes widened.

It was a Marshfield Lake Middle School basketball team jacket.

A boy? Was it possible that the oh-so-perfect Nola had a boy in the house?

Kaitlyn looked again. There was no doubt about it. It was definitely a boy's sleeve.

Kaitlyn's heart began to beat fast. Nola had just broken the number one rule of babysitting. If Kaitlyn told the Baileys, they would never let Nola sit for them again. And of course, they would tell other parents. Nola's babysitting reputation would be ruined for good.

It was perfect.

There was just one teeny-weeny problem. How was Kaitlyn going to explain what she was doing in the Baileys' rosebushes?

As Kaitlyn pondered what to do, the boy took a step forward, and his face came into view.

Kaitlyn gasped. Topher? What was *he* doing here?

Topher turned. Now his back was to the window. Kaitlyn moved so close that her nose was almost pressed against the glass. If only she could hear what he was saying!

Although she couldn't hear Topher, she could see Nola's face. Nola was laughing.

Topher was saying funny things to Nola! Kaitlyn wondered if they were the same funny things he'd said to her. Maybe he was telling her the story of the free-throw shot and the bee (or was it *ears*?) right now.

Kaitlyn felt ill. It was obvious now that Topher and Nola were together. What other explanation could there be for his coming over while she was babysitting?

Kaitlyn didn't want to see any more. She wanted to get far away from them as fast as possible. She fumbled for her cell phone. She needed to call Maggie and Liesel —

Liesel!

Frantically, she checked her watch. It was twenty minutes to eight. How had it gotten so late? She had to get to the museum *now*!

Kaitlyn scrambled out of the bushes. In her hurry, she stepped on Brutus's tail. The dog let out a high-pitched yelp.

Automatically, Kaitlyn glanced toward the kitchen window — and froze. Nola was looking out!

Sheer adrenaline propelled Kaitlyn around the side of the house. A second later, she was out on the street, her heart pounding so hard she thought it might burst.

Had Nola seen her? She couldn't be sure. Kaitlyn had been standing in the shadows. But it had seemed as if Nola was looking right at her.

Kaitlyn decided she didn't have time to worry about it now. She had to get into the city.

Kaitlyn checked her wallet. Eighteen dollars. She hoped it would be enough. Quickly, she scrolled through the numbers in her cell phone, until she found a taxicab company. She gave the cab dispatcher the address of a house a few doors down from the Baileys'.

It seemed to take the cab forever to come. While she waited, Kaitlyn listened to the messages that had come in on her cell phone. There was one from Maggie, wanting to know if she needed a ride. Then one from Liesel, making sure she had the time right. Then another from Maggie. And another from Liesel.

"Where are you?" they both asked.

With each message, Kaitlyn grew more and more frantic. When the taxi finally pulled up, the driver peered out the window at her white, strained face. "Don't tell me you're going to the bus station?" he said.

"No," Kaitlyn said, climbing into the backseat. "Art museum."

The man nodded and put the car into gear. "Good. For a minute there, I thought maybe you were running away."

At a quarter to nine, they pulled up in front of the art museum. "That'll be seventeen fifty," said the cabdriver.

Kaitlyn handed him all the money in her wallet, then got out quickly before he could complain about the stingy tip.

She raced up to the front entrance. But when she tried to open the door, it was locked.

Kaitlyn peered through the tall glass windows. Were there people inside? She couldn't tell. The main entrance hall was dark.

Kaitlyn jiggled the door handle again. Maybe

she had the wrong entrance. She began to circle the building, searching for another door. Near the Dumpster at the back, she found a small unmarked door. It didn't look like a door you'd use to go to a show, but she tried it anyway. It was locked, too.

As Kaitlyn circled back around to the front, she passed the parking lot. Kaitlyn stopped.

The parking lot was empty.

If there were no cars that meant there were no people inside. And if there were no people inside, that meant the show was over. She'd missed it.

Kaitlyn sank down until she was sitting on the curb. The events of the evening played through her mind. How could she have been spying — spying! — on Nola, when her best friend needed her? How had everything gotten so out of hand?

Liesel must hate me, Kaitlyn thought.

And then she thought, *I can't really blame her.*

A siren sounded in the distance. Suddenly Kaitlyn realized where she was — alone, in the city, at night. And she didn't have any way to get home.

She checked her wallet, but she already knew it was empty. There wasn't even enough left for bus fare.

She didn't have a choice. She was going to have to call her parents to come pick her up.

And when they did, they were going to kill her.

Chapter Fifteen

Kaitlyn was grounded. Big-time grounded. Grounded like she had never been grounded before. Actually, she never had been grounded before. But she was sure making up for that now.

"So let me get this straight," her father said on the car ride home from the museum. "You weren't actually sitting for the Baileys tonight. You asked your mother to drop you off at their house, and then you remembered Liesel's art show downtown and decided to take a cab into the city, at night, without telling anyone where you were going."

"Yes," Kaitlyn peeped miserably.

"And explain to me again why you went to the Baileys if you weren't babysitting for them," her father said in an efficient, be-so-kind-as-to-enlighten-me tone that made Kaitlyn nervous.

Kaitlyn had promised herself she wouldn't lie. Lying was what had gotten her into this mess in the first place. So she told her father the truth — most of it, anyway.

"Well, it's like this. There's this other babysitter, Nola, and she's been stealing my business. So I thought I'd go by to sort of, you know, check up on her." She didn't mention the part about hiding in the Baileys' rosebushes. She figured there were certain aspects of the truth her parents didn't need to know.

"It was really stupid, Dad, I know," she added tearfully.

Her father was unmoved. "And what did Nola say when you showed up at the Baileys' house?"

"Well . . . nothing." Nola hadn't said anything when — or if — she'd seen Kaitlyn. "She was sort of . . . *occupied* at the time."

Kaitlyn toyed with the idea of telling her father that Nola had invited Topher over. But one look at her dad's face made Kaitlyn change her mind. Mr. Sweeney was staring straight ahead at the road, his lips pressed together in a tight line. Clearly her father was far more concerned with Kaitlyn's alleged crimes than he was with Nola's.

When they got home, Kaitlyn found her mother waiting for her. She was sitting on the couch, arms folded across her chest, looking angrier than Kaitlyn had ever seen her. The first words out of her mouth were "You're grounded."

"But . . ." Kaitlyn began. Wasn't her mother even going to give her a chance to explain?

"We'll discuss it tomorrow," her father said wearily.

Kaitlyn's parents sent her to her room. They wouldn't even tell her how long she was grounded. *They're probably still trying to determine the exact sentence for each of my heinous crimes,* Kaitlyn thought. She could picture them sitting at the kitchen table, discussing it.

"For starters, she lied to us," her father might say. "That's six months right there."

"Add two years for acting sneaky and dishonest," her mother would insist.

"She let her competitive side get the best of her," her father would add, getting up to pace the room. "That's another five years."

Her mother would nod. "And she went into the city alone —"

"— at night —"

"— without telling anyone where she was going —"

"— without taking enough money and without making any plans for getting back home."

"That's it!" her mother would shout, pounding a spoon on the table like a gavel. "I hereby declare that Kaitlyn Sweeney will be grounded for the rest of her natural-born life!"

Kaitlyn sat in her room, dialing and redialing Maggie's and Liesel's numbers. But there was never an answer. She could picture her friends out with their parents, celebrating with milk shakes and root-beer floats at their favorite diner. She should have been with them. But she wasn't.

Sometime around midnight, Kaitlyn fell into an uneasy slumber.

She woke early the next morning. For a moment, she wondered why she was still in her clothes from the night before and why there was a terrible feeling of dread hanging over her. The events of the evening came flooding back to her.

She took an extra-long shower, delaying going downstairs as long as possible. When she finally walked into the kitchen, she found her parents sitting at the table with cups of coffee. They looked like they hadn't slept very well.

"Sit down, Kaitlyn," her father said.

Kaitlyn was hungry. She had missed dinner the night before and would have liked to get a bowl of cereal. But she sat.

"We've decided to ground you for two months," her father told her.

Kaitlyn did a quick calculation. Two months would be June, almost the end of the school year. Her throat ached like she might cry. She was grounded for the last two months of seventh grade. Granted, it wasn't the rest of her natural-born life — but it was practically the same thing!

"And we're taking your cell phone away," her mother added.

Kaitlyn's eyes widened. Her cell phone! But then how was she going to babysit?

Her mother answered the question before she could even ask it. "No babysitting while you're grounded, either. It seems to me you've let competition with this Nola get out of hand. I think you need to take a break from sitting for a while."

Take a break? Didn't her parents understand that in two months Nola would take over her entire turf? They couldn't do this to her! It was so unfair!

But from the looks on her parents' faces, she could tell it was pointless to argue.

"Do you have anything you want to say?" her father asked.

Kaitlyn knew there was only one thing they wanted to hear: "I'm sorry."

Her parents must've been slightly mollified, because they allowed her one phone call. (*Just like in the movies,* Kaitlyn thought. *They always let you have one phone call before they lock you up forever.*) She used it to call Liesel.

But the phone just rang and rang. Liesel either wasn't home or she wasn't answering the phone.

For the rest of Saturday morning, Kaitlyn moped around the house. She didn't feel happy anywhere. When she was watching TV, she wanted to be in her room. When she was in her room, she felt bored and trapped. She went to the kitchen and opened all the cupboards, but couldn't find anything she wanted to eat.

She worried about Nola stealing her jobs. She worried about Liesel being mad at her. She worried about her parents never trusting her again.

"Do you want to play Monopoly?" Lily asked as Kaitlyn was flipping through the channels for the second time.

"No," said Kaitlyn.

"You can be the dog, and I'll be the shoe," Lily offered gallantly. They both liked the dog playing piece the best. Kaitlyn could tell Lily was trying to cheer her up.

She closed her eyes and sighed. *Why not play*

with Lily? she thought. *It's not like I have anything better to do — for the next two months.*

"All right," she said, opening her eyes. "Go get the board set up."

Lily ran off, hardly believing her luck. Just then, the phone rang. Kaitlyn pounced on it before anyone else could answer.

It was Maggie.

"I've been trying your cell all morning. Why is it turned off?" she asked Kaitlyn.

"My parents took it away when they grounded me," Kaitlyn admitted.

"Grounded you? Kaitlyn, what's going on?"

Kaitlyn felt hot tears at the backs of her eyes. She was dying to talk to someone. So she told Maggie everything: about how she'd spied on Nola and seen Topher, about her cab ride into the city and finding the museum locked, about her parents picking her up and how furious they had been. It all sounded crazy, even to her own ears. But if anyone would understand, it was Maggie.

"And now I'm grounded for two months!" she complained. "That's almost until the end of the school year. And they won't even let me babysit. In two months, Nola will have probably taken over all my jobs!"

She waited for Maggie to say, "That's so wrong!" But there was silence on the other end of the line.

"I can't believe you," Maggie said at last. "Liesel was so excited about the show. She kept saying, 'Where's Kaitlyn?' She waited and waited for you, and you totally let her down. And *still* all you can talk about is Nola."

Kaitlyn swallowed hard. She had expected Maggie to make her feel better, not worse.

In a small voice, she asked, "Um, how was the show?"

"If you'd been there, you would know," Maggie snapped.

"Kaitlyn! Off the phone. Now!" her mother bellowed in the background.

Busted! "I have to go," she told Maggie.

For once, she was actually relieved to get off the phone.

Chapter Sixteen

On Monday morning, Kaitlyn got to school early. She waited by Liesel's locker.

Kaitlyn had tried calling Liesel twice on Sunday while her parents were at the grocery store. The first time, she'd gotten voice mail, but the second time, Liesel had picked up. As soon as she realized it was Kaitlyn, she hung up.

When Liesel saw Kaitlyn standing at her locker, her face went blank. For a second, Kaitlyn thought she was going to turn and walk right back out of the school.

"Excuse me," Liesel said, as if Kaitlyn were a stranger who was standing in her way. She tried to move around Kaitlyn to get to her locker.

"I know you're mad at me," Kaitlyn said. "I just

wanted to say I'm really sorry for missing your art show on Friday."

Liesel folded her arms and looked away.

"Everything's been a little crazy lately," Kaitlyn went on. "I know I let this babysitting stuff get out of hand. But," she added, "I was really doing it to help you."

Liesel's gaze snapped back to Kaitlyn. "What are you talking about?"

"I didn't think you'd save the money for Wonder World," Kaitlyn confessed. "So I thought if I could earn enough for both of us, then we could still all go."

"*Excuse* me?" Liesel didn't look quite as grateful as Kaitlyn had expected her to be.

"That's why I've been so worried about Nola stealing my jobs. I was trying to help you," she said again.

"You think I'm some kind of *charity* case?" Liesel's voice rose with each word.

"Well, I —"

"Spare me, Kaitlyn. I don't need your pity. And I don't need your money. And I definitely don't need your stupid trip to Wonder World!"

"Liesel, I —"

"I don't have anything else to say to you," Liesel

snarled. "Now get out of my way. I'm going to be late for class."

Kaitlyn got out of the way.

At lunchtime, Kaitlyn couldn't find either Liesel or Maggie. They weren't at their lockers, and when Kaitlyn got to the cafeteria, they weren't sitting at their usual table, either. Kaitlyn finally spotted them with a group of girls from the cross-country team. Right away the message was clear: They didn't want to sit with Kaitlyn.

It was like that every day for the rest of the week. Maggie and Liesel sat with the track team or the volleyball team or kids from Liesel's art classes, while Kaitlyn sat alone at their usual table. She didn't know where else to sit. Suddenly she realized how much she'd depended on Liesel and Maggie. They weren't just her best friends — they were her only friends.

Only now they weren't her friends at all.

A few times during that week, Kaitlyn met Nola's eye in the cafeteria. Nola usually sat by herself, too. Kaitlyn wondered why she didn't sit with Topher. Then again, she reasoned, Topher usually sat with the basketball players, and he and Nola were clearly keeping their relationship a secret.

Whenever she saw Nola glance in her direction, Kaitlyn quickly looked away. She figured Nola had noticed that Maggie and Liesel weren't hanging out with her anymore, though. *She's probably laughing about it behind my back,* Kaitlyn thought.

By Friday, Liesel was still giving Kaitlyn the silent treatment. Maggie, who couldn't hold a grudge, had finally started talking to her, but only when Liesel wasn't around.

"You have to make it up to her," Maggie advised Kaitlyn as they walked to class.

"How?" Kaitlyn asked. "I mean, she won't talk to me at school. She won't take my phone calls. What else can I do?"

Maggie shook her head. She didn't know, either. Liesel could hold a grudge forever.

Kaitlyn thought and thought. After school that day, she asked her mother to drive her to a special store where they sold picture frames. Kaitlyn picked out one with gold paint dry-brushed over rough wood. It reminded her of Liesel, the way she could be pretty and rough at the same time.

The frame was expensive. It used up almost half of her Wonder World savings. But Kaitlyn figured it didn't matter, since the trip was off now, anyway.

Afterward, they drove to Liesel's house. Mrs.

Sweeney waited in the car while Kaitlyn rang the doorbell. She felt weird standing at the front door like a stranger, instead of going in through the kitchen like she usually did.

Liesel opened the door.

Kaitlyn said, "I can't stay long." Then she realized Liesel hadn't invited her in.

Taking a breath, Kaitlyn rushed through the rest of her speech. "I just wanted to say again that I'm sorry for missing your show and I miss being your friend and I wanted you to have this." She held out the frame.

Liesel looked at it like it was an object from outer space.

Kaitlyn's heart sank. "It's for your painting," she added.

Was it her imagination, or did Liesel's expression soften? She took the frame out of Kaitlyn's hands and studied it.

Finally, she looked back at Kaitlyn. "Thanks," she said.

"You're welcome," said Kaitlyn. She wanted to say more, but she didn't want to push her luck. "Well, I guess I'll see you at school."

"See you," Liesel said, and closed the door.

Did she like it? Kaitlyn wondered as she walked back to the car. She couldn't really tell from Liesel's reaction. Still, it had gotten Liesel to say a few words to her.

It seemed like a start.

That evening after dinner, Kaitlyn was doing her homework at the kitchen table when the phone rang. Her mother answered it.

"She can't come to the phone right now," Kaitlyn heard her mother say. "May I ask who's calling?"

Kaitlyn's heart lurched hopefully. Was it Liesel? Had she decided to forgive Kaitlyn? Was she calling to make up?

Oh, please! she silently begged her mother. *Please let me take just this one call!*

To her amazement, her mother handed her the phone. She had a funny look on her face. "It's Mrs. Marshfield," she told Kaitlyn.

Kaitlyn stared at her. Mrs. Marshfield, as in Marshfield Lake? The one who lived in the mansion up on the hill? Who was usually only seen rolling through town in her chauffeured Mercedes-Benz?

Kaitlyn took the phone. "Hello?"

"Hello, Kaitlyn? This is Mrs. Marshfield." Kaitlyn was surprised by her voice. She'd expected Mrs. Marshfield to have an exotic accent, or roll all her *R*s, or something. But she sounded just like a normal person.

124

"I'm looking for a babysitter for tomorrow night," Mrs. Marshfield went on. "I'm sorry it's such short notice, but unfortunately our nanny just quit, and it seems the grocery store is fresh out of new nannies." Mrs. Marshfield chuckled at her own joke, then added seriously, "Mr. Marshfield and I have a very important benefit that we cannot miss."

Kaitlyn glanced over at her mother. She was watching with great interest.

"I've made some calls, and you have very good references," Mrs. Marshfield said. "So, are you available?"

Kaitlyn couldn't believe this was happening. This was the ultimate babysitting job, the gig to end all gigs. Only there was just one little problem: She was still grounded.

"Can you hold on a minute, Mrs. Marshfield?" She covered the receiver with her hand. "She wants me to sit tomorrow night!" she whispered to her mother.

Mrs. Sweeney's eyebrows almost shot off her forehead. "Oh?"

"Can I just this once, Mom? Please? You can ground me for an extra week! Just let me take this job." Kaitlyn had never thought she'd have to beg her mother to let her babysit — her mom had always *wanted* her to take the jobs. Then again, a lot of things she'd never expected had happened recently.

Mrs. Sweeney nodded. She looked impressed. "I suppose it would be all right just this once."

"Thank you!" Kaitlyn whispered. "I can do it," she told Mrs. Marshfield.

"Good. Come over at six. Shall I give you our address?"

"That's okay," Kaitlyn said. "I know where you live. Um, by the way, Mrs. Marshfield, how did you get my name?"

"From your flyer," said Mrs. Marshfield. "It's a very nice flyer, although it doesn't mention a price. How would this be?" She named a price that was more than triple Kaitlyn's normal fee.

Kaitlyn swallowed. "That would be fine," she said.

"See you tomorrow night," Mrs. Marshfield said.

Kaitlyn got off the phone feeling better than she had in days. This was it! Her big chance. She was finally going to prove that she was still the best babysitter in town.

Chapter Seventeen

The house was even bigger than Kaitlyn had imagined it would be. As her father drove up the Marshfields' long, winding driveway, it seemed to loom larger and larger. *It looks more like a hotel than a place where people live,* Kaitlyn thought.

"Now, remember to call us if you need anything," Kaitlyn's father said as he pulled up in front of the house.

"Don't worry, Dad. I'll be fine," Kaitlyn assured him. Her parents were acting like this was her first babysitting job ever. They had even given back her cell phone for the occasion. "For emergencies," her mother said. Kaitlyn thought that was funny, since the Marshfields undoubtedly had a phone or two in their house. But she hadn't argued.

"Bye, Dad." Kaitlyn gave her father a kiss on the cheek and got out of the car.

At the front door, Kaitlyn deliberated between the large brass knocker and the doorbell. Finally she chose the bell. It sounded like someone had struck a gong inside.

Mrs. Marshfield answered the door. She was wearing a long black gown and diamond earrings. At least, Kaitlyn thought they were diamonds, though she'd never seen real diamonds that big before.

"Kaitlyn!" Mrs. Marshfield said. "Come on in." She turned and led Kaitlyn into the house, trailing perfume. Kaitlyn tried not to gawk at the high ceilings or the fountain in the entryway.

They entered a living room with a huge fireplace made out of different colored stones. On one wall, a reality show was playing on a thirty-inch flat-screen TV.

I'll bet they have a zillion cable channels, Kaitlyn thought. She was looking forward to finding out after the kids went to bed.

A man in a tuxedo was sitting on a white sofa in front of the television, drinking a glass of something foamy. "Roger, this is Kaitlyn, the babysitter," Mrs. Marshfield told him.

Mr. Marshfield glanced at her and muttered

something that might have been "hello." With a grimace, he went back to his drink.

"Mr. Marshfield has to take antacid before we go to these dinners. The food doesn't always agree with him," Mrs. Marshfield explained to Kaitlyn with a little laugh. Mr. Marshfield harrumphed. Kaitlyn thought Mrs. Marshfield seemed a lot nicer than Mr. Marshfield.

"And here are the kids," Mrs. Marshfield said as a boy and a girl sidled into the room. "Hunter, Marielle, this is Kaitlyn."

Hunter looked like he was about seven. He was brown-haired and plump. Marielle was whip-thin, with hair so blond it was almost white, and she looked a little older. Maybe eight, Kaitlyn thought. She would hardly have guessed they were brother and sister if not for their pointy chins and their eyes, which were huge and green.

"Hi, guys," Kaitlyn said, giving them a big smile. They both smiled back.

"We'd better get going," Mrs. Marshfield said. "My cell phone number is on the pad by the phone, but please don't use it unless it's a real emergency."

"Got it," said Kaitlyn.

"Oh, one other thing, Kaitlyn," Mrs. Marshfield said as she slipped into the coat Mr. Marshfield held out for her. "We never raise our voices in this house. I don't believe in scolding children. We want Hunter and Marielle to grow up feeling confident and loved."

"No problem," said Kaitlyn.

"Good," said Mrs. Marshfield. She kissed each of her kids on the forehead, and in a swirl of perfume and cologne, the Marshfields were gone.

"Well," Kaitlyn said, turning to Hunter and Marielle, "what do you guys want to do?"

"I'm hungry," said Hunter. He had a whiny voice.

"Let's go to the kitchen," Marielle suggested.

"Lead the way," said Kaitlyn. She was looking forward to seeing what kinds of snacks they had in this place!

The kitchen was almost as big as the living room, with marble counters and not one but *two* full-size refrigerators.

"Would you like some lemonade?" Marielle asked Kaitlyn.

"That sounds good," said Kaitlyn. The girl took a pitcher out of one of the refrigerators and poured three glasses.

"We made cupcakes today," Hunter said, reaching for a plastic tub on the counter. "You want one, Kaitlyn?"

"Sure," Kaitlyn said, smiling. She couldn't

believe these kids. They were practically waiting on her hand and foot!

The cupcake Hunter handed her looked delicious. It was chocolate with bright pink frosting. She bit into it hungrily.

Kaitlyn frowned. The cake part tasted good, but there was something weird about the frosting. It was really hard and it wasn't sweet at all. . . .

Suddenly, she noticed that Hunter and Marielle were only pretending to eat their cupcakes. They were using them to hide their smirks.

"Ha-ha!" Hunter burst out. "You just ate glue!"

"And they put horse hooves in glue," Marielle added smartly. "So you just ate horse hooves."

Kaitlyn spit out the bite of cupcake and reached for her lemonade. She took a big swallow to rinse out her mouth.

Ugh! Kaitlyn felt like throwing up. It wasn't lemonade. It was pickle juice!

Hunter and Marielle were practically falling out of their chairs, they were laughing so hard.

Kaitlyn stalked over to the kitchen sink, rinsed out her glass, and refilled it from the tap. As she drank, she glared at the kids over the top of the glass.

Finally they calmed down. "You aren't mad, are you, Kaitlyn?" Marielle said. "It was just a joke."

What could she say? They wanted her to be mad. But she wouldn't give them the satisfaction. "No, I'm not mad," she told them. "I happen to love glue cupcakes."

Hunter snorted. "Yeah, right."

"You really aren't mad, are you?" Marielle asked earnestly. "You still like me, right?"

The poor kid! Kaitlyn thought. No wonder her parents were worried about her self-esteem. "Of course I like you," Kaitlyn told her.

Marielle seemed satisfied. She went to a door at the side of the room and came back a second later with a package of chocolate chip cookies. They happened to be Kaitlyn's favorite kind.

"You want some?" Marielle asked.

Kaitlyn wasn't falling for that again. "No, thanks," she said.

Marielle shrugged and took some cookies. She handed the bag to Hunter, and he took some, too. Kaitlyn watched enviously as they ate their snack.

"I know. Let's play football!" Hunter said, his mouth full of cookies. He and Marielle jumped up from their chairs.

"It's kind of dark outside," Kaitlyn said doubtfully.

The kids were already heading back to the room with the TV. "We don't need to go outside," said

Hunter. He picked up a football from under the coffee table. "We can play right here." He threw the ball at Marielle.

"Whoa, whoa, whoa!" said Kaitlyn, holding up her hands. "I don't think that's a good idea." She could just see the ball flying into the flat-screen TV or one of the huge windows. All her babysitting money wouldn't even *begin* to pay for something like that.

Marielle ignored her. She threw the ball back to Hunter.

"Let's stop now, guys," Kaitlyn pleaded.

Hunter threw the ball to Marielle, harder this time. Marielle returned the pass. But Hunter missed the catch. The ball crashed into a floor lamp, which toppled over.

Kaitlyn raced over and scooped up the ball. Then she went to check the floor lamp. No damage done. She breathed a sigh of relief.

"Give it," said Hunter, reaching for the ball.

"No," said Kaitlyn.

Hunter's face started to redden. Kaitlyn looked around desperately for something to distract them. "Let's . . . let's watch a movie!" she said. The old DVD trick — the question was, would these kids buy it?

Amazingly, they did. "The DVDs are in the den," Marielle said. "I'll go get one."

As Marielle ran off, Kaitlyn caught a glimpse of something moving around outside. Her heart skipped a beat. "There's something out there!" she exclaimed.

Hunter glanced toward the window. "That's just Cornelius."

"Cornelius?" Kaitlyn went to look. A large Saint Bernard puppy sat just outside the door. He was almost entirely white, except for his brown ears and a brown spot on his rump. When he saw Kaitlyn, he wagged his tail.

"We just bought him. He's a show dog. My dad said he cost as much as a horse!" Kaitlyn couldn't tell if Hunter was telling the truth or not. But there was no question that Cornelius was a very pretty puppy.

"He looks cold out there," Hunter said. He looked at Kaitlyn. "We should let him in."

"All right." Kaitlyn unlatched the sliding glass door and pulled it open. Cornelius jumped up on Kaitlyn, almost knocking her over.

"Down. Good dog!" said Kaitlyn.

Cornelius got down. Tail wagging furiously, he ran over and leaped onto the white sofa, leaving a trail of muddy paw prints. From there he jumped onto the coffee table, scattering magazines. He brushed the floor lamp, which fell against the fireplace. The bulb shattered.

Marielle came running back into the room, her hands full of DVDs. "You're not supposed to let the dog in!" she screeched. "He's not trained!"

As if to prove it, Cornelius lifted his leg and let loose on a potted plant.

They spent the next fifteen minutes racing around the house, trying to catch the dog. That is, Kaitlyn tried to catch the dog. Hunter and Marielle mostly just added to the chaos by shouting and egging him on.

By the time she'd managed to shut Cornelius in a bathroom, Kaitlyn was exhausted. Babysitting for the Marshfields was more than she'd bargained for.

But they're just kids, she reminded herself. *Bratty, spoiled kids, but kids nonetheless.* Nothing she couldn't handle.

"How about that movie now, guys?" she said, trying to sound cheerful. She didn't want Hunter and Marielle to think they were wearing her down.

She picked up the stack of DVDs Marielle had brought and thumbed through it. "Wait a second," Kaitlyn said, frowning. "You guys can't watch these. They're all rated R."

"Our dad lets us watch them," Hunter said.

"Yeah, right," said Kaitlyn. "And I'm the queen of France."

Marielle stuck out her lip. "He does too," she insisted. "If you don't believe me, I'll call him right now." She ran over to the phone and started to dial.

"No, no, no!" Kaitlyn said. The Marshfields had said she should only call them in case of an emergency. What would they think if their daughter called to complain that Kaitlyn wasn't letting them watch movies?

"Okay, I'm sure there's something here we can watch." She flipped through the stack again and found one rated PG-13. *Well, I'm thirteen,* Kaitlyn reasoned, *so at least one of us is old enough.* She popped the DVD into the machine.

As the movie started, Kaitlyn slumped down on the couch, grateful to be sitting still for a moment.

"Want a piece of gum?" Marielle asked. She waved a pack with a single piece of gum in front of Kaitlyn's face.

Kaitlyn shook her head. She'd seen that trick before. She would pull on the phony piece of gum and a little wire would spring out and snap her fingers.

Marielle shrugged. She took out the piece of gum, unwrapped it, and popped it into her mouth.

"You have pretty hair, Kaitlyn," she said.

"Thanks," said Kaitlyn, not taking her eyes from the movie. She hoped Marielle would take the hint and settle down to watch.

A moment later, she felt Marielle's fingers stroke her hair. Kaitlyn tensed. But Marielle was gently combing her hair with her fingers.

Kaitlyn remembered that Lily sometimes liked to play hairdresser and comb Kaitlyn's hair. *Maybe Marielle just needs a big sister,* Kaitlyn thought. *Someone who will play with her. Someone she can look up to.*

The feel of Marielle's fingers running through her hair made Kaitlyn feel sleepy. Her eyes started to close.

Suddenly she felt a little tug, as if Marielle's fingers had gotten caught on something. Kaitlyn opened her eyes. Marielle was standing over her. And Kaitlyn didn't like the look on her face.

Slowly, she reached around to feel the back of her head. Her fingers touched a sticky wad.

"Gum? You put gum in my hair?" Kaitlyn shrieked, leaping up off the sofa.

"Please don't raise your voice in our house," Marielle said serenely. On the floor in front of the TV, Hunter was laughing hysterically.

Kaitlyn pressed her lips together. Her nostrils flared. Her fists clenched. It was all she could do to keep from shouting every mean thing she could think of.

Marielle tilted her pointy chin up at Kaitlyn. The look on her face said, *I dare you to say what you're thinking.*

With enormous effort, Kaitlyn got herself under control. She would deal with these brats in a minute. But first things first. Right now she had to save her hair.

Peanut butter. That was supposed to get gum out of hair, wasn't it? Kaitlyn thought she'd heard that somewhere. She couldn't really imagine putting *more* sticky stuff in her hair. But she was willing to try anything.

In the kitchen, Kaitlyn threw open cupboard after cupboard. She found pots, blenders, electric mixers — practically every kitchen appliance you could think of. But where was the food?

"What are you looking for?" Marielle asked. She had followed Kaitlyn into the kitchen.

Kaitlyn ignored her. She glanced around the kitchen, trying to guess where these crazy people stashed their food. Then she remembered: Marielle had gotten the cookies from a door at the side of the room.

She walked over and opened the door. Inside

was a pantry the size of the Sweeneys' entire kitchen. Bottles, jars, cans, and boxes lined the shelves. There was practically a whole grocery store in there!

Kaitlyn walked along one wall, reading the labels. The Marshfields had all kinds of weird food: chestnut paste, balsamic glaze, truffle salt — things Kaitlyn had never heard of before.

She was examining a jar labeled PICKLED HERRING that looked like it belonged in a science lab, when suddenly the door to the pantry slammed shut.

She set down the jar and raced over to the door. It wouldn't budge. Someone had all their weight against it. *Probably Hunter,* she thought. *The tubby little jerk.*

"Not funny, guys!" Kaitlyn said through the door. "Let me out!"

There was the sound of something being dragged across the floor, then a thump as it knocked against the door.

Kaitlyn pushed on the door again. This time it felt different; there was no weight against it, but it was catching on something. Then she understood. They'd jammed a kitchen chair under the door handle.

"All right, guys. That's enough," Kaitlyn said,

trying to sound tolerant and amused. She heard muffled laughing on the other side of the door.

Kaitlyn jiggled the handle. It wouldn't move.

"Hunter? Marielle? Let me out now, okay?"

There was silence.

"Marielle? Hunter? Please let me out." She waited. Nothing. Were they even there?

She pounded on the door. "Let me out or I'm going to tell your parents!"

She heard a noise in another part of the house. It sounded like a small pony was using the living room as a racetrack. Kaitlyn groaned. They'd let the dog out.

Perfect, she thought. *Now the dog is out and I'm locked up.* Considering how things were going, she could only hope Cornelius would be a better baby-sitter than she was.

Kaitlyn banged on the door a few more times, though by now she didn't expect it to help. Finally, she slid down the door and sat on the floor, trying to think what to do.

She heard water rushing through the pipes overhead. Someone had turned on a tap in an upstairs bathroom. *Maybe they're going to give themselves baths and put themselves to bed,* Kaitlyn thought hopefully.

Then again, maybe not.

Panic started to rise in her. She couldn't have the Marshfields come home and find her locked in the pantry and the house in who-knows-what kind of state.

As much as she hated to admit it, she needed help. She pulled out her cell phone, then paused. Who would she call?

911? This didn't exactly qualify as an emergency, Kaitlyn decided. No one was dead or bleeding (at least, she hoped they weren't!), and nothing was on fire — yet. She considered calling her parents.

But they'll never trust me again, she thought.

That left Liesel and Maggie.

Kaitlyn dialed Maggie's number. She got the answering machine.

Liesel and Maggie would be together, Kaitlyn reasoned. If they weren't at Maggie's, that meant they were at Liesel's.

Kaitlyn hesitated. How could she ask Liesel for help when she'd already let her down? What if Liesel laughed in her face?

She had to try anyway. She dialed.

A thudding noise came from overhead. She could have sworn she heard the dog yelp. *What are they doing?*

"Please pick up! Please pick up!" Kaitlyn whispered into the phone.

"Hello?" It was Liesel.

"Liesel, it's Kaitlyn. Don't hang up!"

Liesel was silent.

"Listen, I know I've been a bad friend lately and I let you down in a big way." Kaitlyn was rushing, afraid Liesel would hang up at any moment. "And believe me, I am truly sorry. But right now I really need your help."

As soon as she said it, tears rushed to Kaitlyn's eyes. There was nothing she could do to stop them. It was like all the stress of the last few weeks had finally overflowed.

"I really need you guys right now," Kaitlyn cried into the phone. "Please come help me. Please, Liesel, I need your help!"

Chapter Eighteen

Liesel was silent for a moment. "Where are you?" she asked finally.

Kaitlyn sniffled. "I'm babysitting at the Marshfields' mansion. I'm locked in a pantry off the kitchen."

"What?"

"Listen, these kids are —" Kaitlyn searched for the right word. "Brats" didn't even begin to cover it. "— evil. There's no telling what they're doing right now. I'm serious. I can't do this alone."

There was another pause. "Okay," Liesel said. "We'll be over as soon as we can. Don't go anywhere."

If she hadn't been so freaked out, Kaitlyn would have laughed. "Believe me," she said. "I won't."

For the next half hour, Kaitlyn sat on the floor of

the pantry, listening to the sinister noises overhead. There were lots of sloshing, some scrambling sounds, and a crash that sent chills down Kaitlyn's spine.

She tried to imagine what Marielle and Hunter were doing. Then she tried very hard *not* to imagine what they were doing. Whatever it was, it couldn't be good.

A sound like a gong rang through the house. *What now?* Kaitlyn thought. Then she remembered. That was the sound the doorbell made.

The doorbell rang again. There was a pause. Kaitlyn pressed her ear to the pantry door. She heard the sound of footsteps echoing in the entranceway. The noises were still coming from overhead, which meant that whoever was at the front door had let themselves in.

Either Maggie and Liesel are here, or the place is being robbed, Kaitlyn thought. She figured either situation was preferable to the current one.

A moment later, she heard footsteps coming across the kitchen. Kaitlyn scrambled to her feet.

The doorknob jiggled, and a second later, the door swung open. Kaitlyn's cry of relief caught in her throat. Before her stood Liesel, Maggie ... and Nola.

"What's *she* doing here?" Kaitlyn asked.

"You said you needed help," Maggie replied in her don't-argue-with-me voice. "And *we* don't know anything about babysitting."

Kaitlyn was about to say something mean, but then thought better of it. She really was in no position to argue. "How did you get in?" she asked instead.

"The front door was unlocked," Nola said. The tone of her voice implied that she, Nola, would never leave a front door open while she was babysitting. Kaitlyn dared her with her eyes to say more. Amazingly, Nola kept quiet.

Just then, Maggie's gaze fell on the roomful of food behind Kaitlyn. "Wow, check this place *out!*"

"Believe me," said Kaitlyn, "it's not as good as it looks."

"Where are the kids?" Liesel asked.

"Somewhere upstairs, I think," Kaitlyn said. "Now listen, we have to do this carefully. They're vicious and they may be armed — slingshots, water guns, who knows what else. But we have the element of surprise on our side."

The other girls nodded.

"Oh, and one other thing," Kaitlyn said. "You can't raise your voice or scold them in any way."

"What?" cried Nola.

"It's the Marshfields' rule."

Nola looked like she wanted to spit. "That's no rule! That's just plain bad parenting."

Kaitlyn looked at her with surprise. It had never occurred to her that she might go against what the Marshfields had told her.

"Everybody ready?" she asked.

They were. Together, the four girls crept up the stairs. On the second floor, light came from under a door at the end of the hall. They heard the dog whimpering on the other side.

With silent nods, the girls sneaked up to the door. "On the count of three," Kaitlyn whispered. "One, two, *three!*"

They burst into the room. Hunter and Marielle were crouched in the middle of a black marble bathroom floor. They were holding Cornelius between them.

Kaitlyn could feel herself starting to hyperventilate. They had painted the dog — the very expensive, purebred show dog — purple. Empty jars of purple paint were tipped over on the floor.

Maggie saw Kaitlyn start to freak. She put a hand on her arm.

"Stop!" Nola bellowed at the kids. "Step away from the dog!"

Marielle squinted up at her. "Who're you?" she said nastily.

Nola put her hands on her hips. In a voice at least an octave lower than her normal one, she said, "I'm the new babysitter."

If Kaitlyn hadn't known better, she would have sworn she saw flames shoot out of Nola's eyes.

"Now get up, you spoiled little brats, and get this bathroom cleaned up," Nola commanded.

Hunter recovered from his surprise long enough to sneer, "Make me."

Nola put her face so close to his that their noses almost touched. "Little boy," she purred, "you don't want me to make you."

Hunter's eyes widened.

Nola began barking orders in a way that would have put an army general to shame. Even Kaitlyn was a little intimidated. She'd had no idea Nola had it in her.

When the kids' backs were to them, Nola turned and winked at Kaitlyn.

Kaitlyn got it. Nola had the kids under control. Kaitlyn turned to Maggie and Liesel. "Maggie, you go downstairs and start cleaning up the living room. See if you can find some upholstery cleaner and get those paw prints off the couch."

Maggie started out the door.

"Oh, and Maggie?" said Kaitlyn.

"Yeah?"

"Don't eat the cupcakes. They're poisoned."

Maggie looked at Kaitlyn in horror. She turned and left the room.

"Now," Kaitlyn said to Liesel, "what are we going to do about Cornelius?"

They watched the dog shake himself. Drops of purple paint flew everywhere. Kaitlyn was grateful that most of the surfaces in the bathroom were black.

"What color did he used to be?" Liesel asked.

"White mostly, with brown ears." Kaitlyn's chest felt tight.

Liesel picked up one of the empty jars of paint from the floor. "Don't worry, he'll be white with brown ears again," she told Kaitlyn. "It's tempera paint. Water-based. It should wash right out."

Kaitlyn could have hugged her. But Liesel was already over at the bathtub taps, filling the Jacuzzi tub with water.

Kaitlyn grabbed Cornelius's collar and dragged him over to the tub. Together, the two girls managed to get him in. Cornelius scrambled, splashing water everywhere. But Kaitlyn held him firmly as Liesel started to squirt expensive shampoo over his coat.

Kaitlyn watched as Liesel began to soap the dog's head. "Liesel?"

"Hmm?"

"Thanks for coming."

Liesel studied her for a second. Then she smiled. "What are friends for?"

Two hours later, the house looked almost as good as it had when Kaitlyn had walked in the door. The magazines were artfully scattered on the coffee table. The bulb in the floor lamp was replaced. The paw prints were just faint gray stains on the white sofa. Kaitlyn had to get her nose right up to the fabric to see them.

It had taken three shampoos and nearly an hour with the blow-dryer, but Cornelius was as white and fluffy as he had been at the beginning of the night. What's more, he adored Kaitlyn. He kept trying to lick her face while she blow-dried him.

Hunter and Marielle were in bed, their faces washed and their teeth brushed. Kaitlyn guessed they probably weren't sleeping, but she didn't really care as long as they stayed in their rooms. She didn't know what Nola had said to them, but whatever it was, it had worked.

Maggie was scrubbing at one last paw print when they heard a car pull up the driveway.

"Quick! Out the back!" Kaitlyn said, ushering Maggie, Liesel, and Nola to the back door. The girls slipped outside and Kaitlyn latched the door behind them.

Kaitlyn flung herself onto the sofa and flicked on the TV. She skidded through the channels, looking for something appropriately innocuous. Ice-skating. Perfect.

The front door opened. She could hear Mr. and Mrs. Marshfield's voices echoing in the cavernous front hallway.

"I cannot believe you called Harold Hartman 'Hal,'" Mr. Marshfield snapped. "For Pete's sake, Deborah, he's the most important man in the state!"

"Well, he *looks* like a Hal," Mrs. Marshfield shot back.

When they walked into the living room, they seemed surprised to see Kaitlyn sitting calmly in front of the television.

"Where are the kids?" Mrs. Marshfield asked. She looked around the living room, as if she thought Kaitlyn had stuffed them behind some furniture.

"They're in bed, of course," Kaitlyn replied, getting up from the couch. "I hope you had a nice evening," she added pleasantly.

"Oh, we did," Mrs. Marshfield said, glaring at her husband. He was already watching TV and didn't seem to notice. "Well, it seems everything here is in perfect shape." Mrs. Marshfield sounded like she couldn't really believe it.

"Yep, it seems to be." Kaitlyn couldn't really believe it herself.

"Is it midnight already?" Mrs. Marshfield asked, checking her watch. "I guess I owe you for six hours." She counted out the bills and handed them to Kaitlyn. "And I guess you'll need a ride home. I'll call the chauffeur."

"No, no, that's all right," said Kaitlyn. "I've already got a ride."

"Well, Kaitlyn, it was nice meeting you," Mrs. Marshfield said as she walked Kaitlyn to the door. "Thank you for coming on such short notice. Maybe you'll sit for us again sometime?"

Fat chance! thought Kaitlyn. She wouldn't set foot in this house again for all the money in the world!

But she just smiled sweetly. "Maybe," she said. "Bye, Mrs. Marshfield."

Chapter Nineteen

Kaitlyn walked slowly down the Marshfields' long, curving driveway. She wanted to take her time getting to the bottom. She had a lot to think about before she faced her friends.

To begin with, there were the Marshfields. Kaitlyn wasn't impressed by them anymore. Sure, their house was big and full of nice things. But she wouldn't have traded places with anyone who lived there.

And Liesel and Maggie: They'd showed up like heroes when she had needed them. Kaitlyn was pretty sure that meant they were friends again. But she didn't want to take it for granted.

Then there was Nola. Kaitlyn didn't know what to make of her. She had helped Kaitlyn out with no questions asked. And she hadn't acted snotty or like she was trying to show Kaitlyn up. She seemed glad to help.

Was it possible that Kaitlyn had gotten so caught up in the war with Nola that she hadn't even noticed there wasn't really a war going on?

Kaitlyn came to the end of the driveway. Nola, Liesel, and Maggie were waiting for her at the bottom.

"How'd it go?" Maggie asked anxiously.

Kaitlyn shook her head. "They called the cops. We're all going to juvie." She briefly enjoyed their looks of shock. Then she grinned. "I'm just joking. They didn't suspect a thing."

Liesel punched her in the arm. "That's not funny. For a second, I thought you were serious."

"I might be," Kaitlyn pointed out. "I'm not sure what Mr. and Mrs. Marshfield will do when their kids tell them what really happened."

"Don't worry," Nola said. "I took care of that."

"How?" Kaitlyn asked, surprised.

Nola smiled. "I told them that if they breathed a word about this to their parents, I'd make sure I got a job as their *permanent* nanny."

They all laughed.

Kaitlyn took the money Mrs. Marshfield had

given her out of her pocket and divided it into four equal shares. She handed it out.

Liesel's eyes widened. "Wow. If this is what you get paid, I'm totally going to reconsider babysitting."

Kaitlyn shook her head. "Not all jobs are like this one."

"Thank goodness," Nola added. She and Kaitlyn both laughed.

How weird is this? thought Kaitlyn. *I'm standing at the bottom of the Marshfields' driveway, having a friendly conversation with Nola.* A day ago she would never have thought it possible. Liesel and Maggie were looking back and forth between them like they weren't sure what to make of it, either.

"Well," said Kaitlyn, "I guess we should go home. How did you guys get here?"

"Liesel and I rode our bikes," Maggie said. She pointed to two bikes leaning against a lamppost. "Nola met us here."

"I live just a few blocks away," Nola explained.

"We'll walk you," said Kaitlyn.

The streets were quiet and they walked in silence. Kaitlyn was thinking again.

"This is it," Nola said. They stopped in front of a gray house with white shutters.

Kaitlyn paused. "Can I talk to you for a minute, Nola? Alone?"

Nola looked surprised, but she nodded. They moved a few paces away from Liesel and Maggie.

"First off," said Kaitlyn, "thank you."

Nola shrugged. "Don't mention it. I had fun."

"No, seriously," Kaitlyn said. "You saved me in there. You're a really good babysitter."

Nola smiled.

"And . . ." Kaitlyn paused. This was harder than it had been when she'd practiced it in her head. "I owe you an apology. I haven't been very nice to you."

Nola didn't say anything, but Kaitlyn could see from her face that it was true.

"I think I was jealous of you," Kaitlyn admitted.

"Jealous of *me*?" Nola looked stunned.

"Because you're such a good sitter."

"But I've been jealous of *you*," Nola said.

Now it was Kaitlyn's turn to be surprised. "Why?"

"Because everyone in town knows you. And you have all these great friends. Aside from the kids I babysit, the only person who talks to me is my math tutor."

"Math tutor?" Kaitlyn asked.

"Topher Walker. He tutors me in math. I'm really, really bad at math — I almost flunked last year. I was only allowed to graduate to seventh grade if I got a tutor. I didn't want anyone to know. But," she added, "I guess now you know."

Kaitlyn barely registered the last part of what Nola was saying. Her mind was racing. Topher was Nola's math tutor. Was that why he'd been at the Baileys' that night?

"So, um, you and Topher get together and study in the evenings?" Kaitlyn tried to sound casual.

"Mostly right after school," Nola said. "Though one time he dropped off a problem set while I was babysitting. By the way," she added, "thank you for not saying anything to the Baileys about that. I know we're not ever supposed to have boys in the house. "

Kaitlyn froze. So Nola *had* seen her that night!

Nola looked at her curiously. "What were you doing in the Baileys' backyard, anyway?"

"Just, um, looking for something that I lost," Kaitlyn told her. *Like my dignity,* she added to herself.

"Oh. Well, I'm sure they'll call you if they find it. They adore you. They're always saying nice things about you."

"They are?" Kaitlyn asked.

"You know, we should go into business together."

Wow, thought Kaitlyn, *this* is *turning out to be a weird evening.* "Why?" she asked. "You seem to do fine on your own."

"Yeah, but I'm not very organized. A couple of weeks ago, I showed up for a babysitting job almost an hour late. I'd completely gotten the time wrong. Can you believe it? The parents had a fit."

Kaitlyn winced. She really did feel bad about that.

"Anyway, think about it."

"I'll think about it," said Kaitlyn. "Well, see you in school."

"See you," said Nola.

Kaitlyn started to walk back to her friends.

"Hey, Kaitlyn?" Nola said.

Kaitlyn turned. "Yeah?"

Nola looked worried. "I don't know how to tell you this."

Kaitlyn braced herself for the worst.

"You have gum in your hair."

Chapter Twenty

Kaitlyn, Liesel, and Maggie sat around the Sweeneys' kitchen table, eating cherry Popsicles. It was a warm spring afternoon. All the windows in the kitchen were open to let in the fresh air.

"And then Amy said that Josh likes April," Maggie told Kaitlyn.

"No, no," Liesel corrected her. "First she said that Josh likes Jessica. *Then* she said that Josh likes April."

Maggie and Liesel were filling Kaitlyn in on the highlights of the basketball game from the night before. It had been a week since the crazy night at the Marshfields' house, and things were almost back to normal. Normal, but not exactly the same.

Kaitlyn was still grounded, but because she'd

been helping around the house, her parents had decided she could occasionally have friends over. She could even talk on the landline now. Kaitlyn figured it was sort of like getting parole for good behavior.

Kaitlyn shook her head, enjoying the way her new cropped haircut swished against the back of her neck.

"I still can't believe how good it looks," Liesel said.

Kaitlyn smiled. They'd had to cut it really short to get all the gum out. Now it fell to just below her jawline. Everybody at school said it looked super-cute. Except for Topher. He said it looked "*muy bien.*"

"Did you see Topher at the game?" Kaitlyn asked.

Liesel waved her Popsicle. "Yeah. He, you know, made some goals."

"He made two free throws and scored the winning three-point shot," said Maggie, who was better versed in athletic terminology.

Kaitlyn sighed. She wished she could have been there.

"So," said Liesel, "have you thought any more about going into business with Nola?" Kaitlyn had told her friends about Nola's offer.

"Yeah, I've thought about it. But I don't think I'm going to do it."

Maggie frowned. "You're not still grudging, are you? You need to just let it go. Nola's pretty nice. And she really helped you out."

"No, she's cool," Kaitlyn said. For the past week, Nola had been eating lunch with them at the yellow table in the cafeteria. It still bugged Kaitlyn how she sometimes acted like she knew more than everybody else. But she was starting to realize that Nola mostly did it when she was feeling nervous. When she relaxed, she could actually be pretty funny.

"I'm thinking I might give up babysitting altogether," Kaitlyn said.

Liesel's and Maggie's mouths fell open simultaneously. "What do you mean you're thinking about giving up babysitting?" Maggie demanded.

"Don't let Nola push you out," Liesel said with a frown. "I'm sure you can get your jobs back just as soon as you're ungrounded."

"I'm not letting her push me out of it. I *want* to quit."

"But I thought you *loved* babysitting," Maggie said.

Kaitlyn shook her head. "I don't, really. I mean, it was nice to have a way to earn some money. But now I don't really need it since the Wonder World trip is off."

"*What?*" screeched Liesel.

"Who said the Wonder World trip is off?" asked Maggie.

Kaitlyn looked back and forth at her friends, confused. "But I thought . . . Liesel said . . ."

"Forget what I said," Liesel told her. "I'm *counting* on going to Wonder World. My future happiness depends on it."

"But I thought you didn't have any money saved," Kaitlyn asked.

"*Au contraire, mon frere,*" said Liesel. "I have sixty-one dollars."

Kaitlyn gaped at her. "How?"

"Didn't you hear? I got second place in the art show," Liesel said. "A twenty-five-dollar prize. And that got me motivated. I've been helping my mom in her studio, cleaning brushes and stuff. And then there's the money we got from the Marshfields last weekend."

"That's awesome, Liesel. But that means . . ." Kaitlyn thought of all the things she'd spent her money on — the cab to the museum, the frame for Liesel, xeroxing all the flyers. "Well, now *I'm* the one who doesn't have enough," she admitted. "And my parents said I can't babysit while I'm grounded."

"They said you can't babysit, but they didn't say you couldn't do something else," Maggie pointed out.

"Like what?" asked Kaitlyn.

Maggie shrugged. "Mow lawns?"

"Wash cars?" suggested Liesel.

"Weed gardens?"

"Walk dogs?"

"Walk dogs," said Kaitlyn. "Now *that* is not a bad idea."

A gleam started to form in her eye. She could see herself strolling down Lakeside Drive, a pack of happy, well-trained dogs trotting along at her heels. She would be the best dog walker in Marshfield Lake!

The phone rang, jolting her out of her fantasy. Kaitlyn got up to answer it.

"Could I speak to Kaitlyn?" the caller asked.

"Speaking."

"*Hola,* Kaitlyn. It's Topher."

Kaitlyn's heart started to beat faster. "Hey, Topher," she said, forcing her voice to stay calm.

Liesel's and Maggie's heads snapped up. Maggie clamped her hand over her mouth to muffle a squeal.

"So, what's up?" Topher asked.

"Not much," said Kaitlyn. "I'm just hanging out with my friends."

At the table, Liesel was making kissy faces. Kaitlyn threw a Popsicle stick at her.

"Oh, do you have to go?" Topher asked. Was she mistaken, or did he sound disappointed?

"No, no," Kaitlyn said. "What's up?"

"I was calling to see if you had the Spanish homework," Topher said.

Kaitlyn's heart sank. Was that all? *That's probably why he called the last time, too,* she told herself. She'd gotten all worked up over nothing.

She thought for a second. "Señora Ramos didn't give us any homework this weekend."

"Oh. Okay." There was a pause. "Actually, that's not why I'm calling."

Oh?

"I wondered if maybe you wanted to hang out sometime," Topher said.

Oh!

But — *oh no!* "I would love to —" Kaitlyn couldn't believe she had to say this — "but I'm grounded."

"Oh." This time there was no mistake. Topher really did sound disappointed. "What did you get grounded for?" he asked.

Kaitlyn glanced at Liesel and Maggie. They were hanging on every word. "It's a long story," she told Topher.

"I bet you can't tell me the whole story in Spanish," Topher said.

Kaitlyn smiled. "Try me."

"All right, I will." Kaitlyn could tell from his voice that Topher was smiling, too. "I'll call you later tonight."

"Deal."

Maggie and Liesel pounced on her as soon as she was off the phone. "What was all that?" Maggie demanded.

Kaitlyn grinned. "Just a little healthy competition."

By the next day, it was settled. No doubt about it. Charlie was signing up for musical auditions with Nicole. She was trying out for the junior high's production of *Robin Hood* — whether she wanted to or not. They met, as planned, outside the school entrance before homeroom and went upstairs together to sign up. There was the sheet — all eleven by fourteen inches of it — just waiting for their names.

"Hey!" Nicole said. "I don't see Kyle's name here yet."

"Are you sure?" Charlie said.

"Yeah. Take a look."

Charlie's eyes scanned the list of a dozen or so names, most of which she'd never heard of before, and frowned.

"I hope your brother didn't talk him out of it," Nicole said.

"Me, too," Charlie said, as doubt tiptoed through her brain. "I mean, he seemed really serious about it yesterday. . . ."

"Well," said Nicole, trying to stay optimistic, "maybe he just hasn't had a chance yet. It's only the middle of the week."

"Hi, guys!" said a voice from behind them.

Charlie turned and saw Megan and a few more kids from chorus approaching.

"Did you sign up? We're going to, too!"

"Oh, good," said Charlie. "I was getting a little worried that we wouldn't know anyone."

Megan walked up to the list and signed her name. "Well, now you do!" she said. She handed the pen to her friend Claire. "I'm so glad Mr. Matthews told us about the musical. I had no idea."

"*I'm* glad we get extra credit!" said Claire. Then her hand suddenly froze. "You do think he was serious about that, don't you?"

"He'd better be!" said another girl, Lily. "Now hurry up and write your name down."

Soon there were seven more sixth graders on the list, and a bunch more kids waiting to add their names. Arden, another alto like Nicole, handed her the pen. "Your turn," she said. "What role do you want?"

Nicole signed her name. "Well, Maid Marian, of course," she said. "But I'll play anything. Even a boy!" She passed the pen to Charlie. "What about you?"

Charlie laughed and shrugged. "Who knows if I'll get a part at all?"

"Oh, you definitely will," said Megan. "You are *such* a good singer."

"Yeah, you really are," said Claire.

Charlie grinned as she dotted her *i*. "Thanks," she mumbled, suddenly self-conscious but flattered. *You know*, she thought to herself, *even if Kyle doesn't try out, this could be fun. . . .*

"Well, well, well. If it isn't Squeaky Locker Girl! Going to try out for the musical? I hope you sound better than that locker of yours. Or do you plan on torturing us that way, too?"

The dot on Charlie's *i* turned into a long, tortured slash as her hand slipped halfway down the page. She didn't turn around to see who belonged to the haughty voice behind her — or the laughs that followed. She didn't have to.

"Let's see," said Amber Wiley, walking up to the list and elbowing Charlie out of the way. She studied the sign-up sheet closely. "'Charlie Moore.' Oh, sure! You're one of Sean's sisters." She turned and looked at her friends like she'd just smelled something awful. "I think *all* these little sixth graders signed up, guys. Can you believe it? What songs do you think they'll audition with? The Wiggles?"

She gave her friends a second to appreciate her wit, then turned back to Charlie. "*You'll* probably sing one of your brother's lame songs, though, won't you?"

Charlie looked back at Amber without the slightest idea of what to say. The thing was, she agreed with her. Her brother's songs *were* lame. Except maybe for the one about peace and love. She didn't know where that one had come from. But it was pretty good.

"Oh, whatever," said Amber, finally seeming to tire of making fun of Charlie for the moment. "Do you mind?" She held out her hand and tapped her foot impatiently.

Charlie stared back at her blankly.

"The *pen*!" Amber said, as if Charlie were two years old. "I know, you probably don't think I *need* to audition, having starred in the last two shows. But it's a formality. So hand it over. Eighth graders can't be late, you know. Our classes are very important."

More than happy to hand over the pen (and get

as far from Amber as possible), Charlie offered it up willingly and slunk back into the crowd.

"*Thank* you," said Amber, flipping her red hair as she turned to face the sign-up sheet. She added her name to the very top of the growing list.

But Nicole wasn't about to stand back and watch. "You know," she said, stepping up and planting her feet on the floor behind Amber. "There's no need to talk to people that way."

Amber spun around. "Excuse me?" she said, chuckling.

"You heard me," said Nicole.

"No, I didn't," said Amber. Her eyes narrowed. "Say it again. I *dare* you."

Charlie had to grin. *She dares her?* she thought. This was going to be good. Nicole hadn't passed up a dare since second grade.

Nicole put her hands on her hips and made the most of the two inches she had on the older girl. "You," Nicole declared, "are just plain —"

Suddenly, Nicole's jaw went slack — but it wasn't because of Amber.

Like the Red Sea parting, the whole cluster of girls stepped back to allow his royal cuteness, Kyle, to drift through. Their eyes trailed him as he made his way to the list. Even Amber was dumbstruck — for a split second.

"Kyle!" she said, quickly regaining her composure. "Oh, good! Are you signing up, too?"

Kyle shrugged and coolly nodded, taking time to flash a friendly grin at each and every girl around him. "Yeah."

For the first time in her life, Charlie saw real live human eyelashes actually flutter. "We should rehearse together for the audition!" cooed Amber.

Kyle shrugged again. "Yeah, maybe." He looked at the sign-up sheet, then glanced around for a second, saw the pen in Amber's hand, and reached into his pocket. He pulled out a nubby pencil and loosely wrote his name down on the sheet.

"I'll call you!" said Amber, as Kyle began to walk away.

"Yeah," he said. Then, without so much as a warning — without the slightest indication at all — Kyle did something amazing. He stopped in front of Charlie.

"Hey." He smiled and nodded toward the sign-up sheet. "Cool. You signed up."

Through sheer determination, Charlie willed herself not to faint as her stomach, lungs, and liver — and maybe her spleen, too — wedged themselves in her throat.

A horrible thought flashed suddenly through her brain: Could people explode?